"It'll take me only a few minutes to settle in. If you'll show me to your bedroom..."

"My bedroom?" Sara sat up straight in the chair. "Why in the world would you need to see my bedroom?"

Crow heaved an exasperated sigh. "Because that's where I'll be sleeping."

"With me?" Sara's blue eyes flashed.

"No, right outside your door." Crow paused and regarded her thoughtfully. "Disappointed?"

Her eyebrow raised in amused contempt. "Hardly."

Crow smiled to himself. Perhaps he'd been too quick to dismiss the singer as just another pretty face. It seemed she had spunk. This assignment might be more fun than he'd first thought....

Books by Cynthia Rutledge

Love Inspired

Unforgettable Faith #102
Undercover Angel #123
The Marrying Kind #135
Redeeming Claire #151
Judging Sara #157

CYNTHIA RUTLEDGE

lives in the Midwest and has enjoyed reading romance since her teens. She loves the fact that you can always count on a happy ending.

Writing inspirational romance has been especially gratifying because it allows her to combine her faith in God with her love of romance.

Judging Sara is her fifth book for Love Inspired.

Judging Sara
Cynthia Rutledge

Love Inspired®

Published by Steeple Hill Books™

STEEPLE HILL BOOKS

Steeple Hill™

ISBN 0-373-87164-3

JUDGING SARA

Visit us at www.steeplehill.com

Printed in U.S.A.

To Bob and Diane Ziemer,
a favorite police officer and a favorite friend

Chapter One

On a scale of one to ten, Sara Michaels decided James Smith's kiss rated no more than a five. It wasn't a great kiss; her pulse didn't soar and her heart didn't flutter like the heroines in the books she read. But it wasn't bad, either. His lips were cool and dry, and though he kept his mouth firmly closed, he tasted like spearmint-flavored mouthwash.

Impulsively she pulled James against her and returned the kiss with unusual gusto. Normally he kept a proper distance between them and she could sense his surprise when her body molded to his and her arms slipped up to encircle his neck.

He hesitated for only a second before his lips captured hers, more demanding this time. In that moment his rating rose to a six. Sara resisted a sudden impulse to run her fingers through his care-fully coiffed hair or maybe even nuzzle his neck.

Sara stopped herself just in time. She could only imagine his response if she did something so fool-ish. He'd probably think she'd turned into some kind of wanton woman. Straight-as-an-arrow Sara a wanton woman? Laughter bubbled up from deep inside and tugged at the corners of her mouth. Un-expectedly a giggle slipped out.

"Sara?" James broke the contact and took a step back. His brows pulled together and she could see the hurt confusion in his eyes.

Shame flooded Sara. He probably thought she was laughing at him.

"I don't know what got into me." She touched his arm with her hand. "I'm sorry."

James was a wonderful man, an honorable man. A man any woman would be lucky to call her own. The dozen yellow roses sitting on the side table in the crystal vase were a testament to his generosity and thoughtfulness. Even though he knew red was her favorite color, he'd chosen yellow for friend-ship rather than be presumptuous and pick the ones that stood for love.

"Am I interrupting?" Meg Stanley, Sara's man-ager, stood in the doorway, a knowing smile on her face.

"No, of course not. James just stopped by. With

flowers.'' Sara swept a hand in the direction of the coffee table. "Aren't they lovely?"

"Beautiful," Meg said. Though she'd once told Sara she personally didn't care much for James, she graciously cast an admiring glance at the flowers. "You done good, James."

James winced, and Sara knew even though he understood that Meg's grammatical error was intentional, it had still hurt his ear. Sometimes his insistence on perfect grammar got tedious, but he meant well.

Sara's once-abysmal grammar had improved dramatically over the past year, thanks to James's tutelage. Of course, he insisted that, as her publicist, honing her image was just part of his job.

"What brings you by today?" James's gaze narrowed. "I thought you were out of town this weekend."

"I was." Meg dropped her purse to the floor and settled into a nearby chair. "But I got a hot lead on a bodyguard for Sara."

"Bodyguard?" His blond brows slanted in a frown. "I can't believe you're doing all this because of a few ridiculous notes. Don't you think you're overreacting?"

"I'm not overreacting and they're not ridiculous." Meg's blue eyes snapped. "They're threats against Sara. I would think you'd be more concerned. As her publicist, if nothing else."

"That's exactly why I am concerned, Meg." James didn't bother to hide his displeasure.

Here we go again.

Sara took a seat on the Queen Anne sofa and waited for the battle to begin. The two had been arguing steadily about how to handle the matter since the day that Meg had discovered Sara had been receiving threatening notes and called the police.

James had been furious because of the possibility of bad press. Sara had deliberately played it cool. No one could suspect she knew more than she was telling.

The police had said that although the notes were disturbing, they weren't threatening in the legal sense of the word. And that, even if they found the writer, they wouldn't be able to prosecute.

Sara had thought that would be the end of it and Meg would let the matter drop. Obviously she'd been wrong.

"C'mon, Meg." Sara kept her tone light. "Having a bodyguard could cause all sorts of unnecessary talk."

"I agree," James added.

"I agree, too," Meg said.

"You do?" Sara and James spoke as one.

"Of course." Meg's lips curved up in a slight smile. "That's why I thought we'd say he was your new boyfriend."

"Boyfriend?!" Sara's voice came out as a high-pitched squeak.

"Absolutely not." James crossed his arms across his chest and a hint of sheen graced his forehead.

"Okay." Meg shrugged. "Have it your way. I'm not inflexible. If you only want Crow as your bodyguard, that's fine too."

"Crow?" A faint image of a martial arts master flashed through Sara's mind. "You've got to be kidding."

"Tell me you haven't been drinking."

Meg gasped.

"James!" Sara slugged him in the arm. "What in the world has gotten into you?"

Although Meg freely admitted she'd been an alcoholic, James also knew she hadn't had a drink in five years. She'd quit drinking the year before she'd taken over handling Sara's career and she'd been sober since.

"I'm sorry, Meg," James said, sounding remorseful. "I didn't mean it the way it sounded."

"Apology accepted," Meg said smoothly with no expression on her face, but her eyes were stony with anger. "To answer your question. No, I haven't been drinking. And no, I'm not kidding. Not at all."

"I seem to be putting my foot in my mouth a lot today, so I hope you don't take this wrong."

James moved to stand behind Sara and his hand dropped to rest loosely on her shoulder. "But it appears to me that having a bodyguard or not having a bodyguard is Sara's decision, not yours."

"I'm her manager. And her friend." Meg's gaze shifted to Sara. "Unless that's not what you want anymore."

Meg's expression was carefully controlled but her hands were knotted on her lap. Sara knew Meg realized the chance she was taking, pushing the issue.

It was no secret that for months James had been trying to get Sara to move her management contract to a firm run by one of his friends. A firm he said had the ability to make her into a superstar.

"Sara. You don't want this investigation pushed," James said persuasively. "You've told me so yourself."

That much was certainly true. The thought of what such an investigation might uncover turned Sara's blood cold. But the thought of hurting Meg, who'd been more of a mother to her than her own had ever been, was unbearable.

Dear God, please help me.

"Meg is talking bodyguard, James," Sara said finally, flashing a reassuring smile at her manager. "Not a P.I. or a cop. Right, Meg?"

Meg hesitated for a moment and then nodded. "That's right."

"Well, then." Sara smiled brightly. "I don't see any problem. But I'm not sure when I'll be able to meet this Mr. Crow—"

"It's just Crow," Meg interrupted. "And as far as when, why not now?"

"Now?" Sara frowned.

"Now is as good a time as any." Meg rose from the overstuffed chair. "He's in the foyer waiting. I'll go get him."

"He's here?" Sara forced herself to remain calm. She needed to slow things down. The trouble was, she didn't know how to do that without arousing suspicion. Still, he *was* only a bodyguard. And he would be working for her.

"You certainly didn't waste any time getting this all arranged," James said.

A self-satisfied smile crossed Meg's face. "Sara pays me to keep on top of things."

He stiffened as though Meg had struck him.

Sara hid a smile. One of James's selling points for the new firm was that they'd keep on top of the changes in the industry. But in the year he'd been her publicist, he'd never taken the time to get to know Meg. Or to give her any credit.

In Sara's mind, there wasn't a better manager in the business. And it didn't surprise her in the least that Meg had come with all her ducks in a row, fully prepared.

"What are we waiting for?" Sara said. "Bring him in."

Salvadore "Crow" Tucci shifted uncomfortably on the rock-hard settee and glanced down at his watch.

The fifteen minutes of waiting had been pure torture. Unlike many guys who could sit in a recliner all afternoon watching football, Crow needed activity—the more physical the better.

That's why he'd chosen law enforcement after graduating from college instead of becoming a physician like his brother Nick, or a lawyer like his other brother Tony.

At first his parents had been supportive. But when he'd gotten promoted and gone undercover, all that changed. His mother's fears skyrocketed out of control. She was certain every time he took an assignment that his cover would be blown and he'd get shot. His father worried more about him adopting a new identity for weeks or months than he did about the physical danger.

Crow had dismissed these concerns. And for the first three years he had little difficulty separating his personal life from the life he led as an undercover cop. But recently he'd noticed a subtle shift. He'd started to feel more like Crow than Sal. He'd become suspicious and cynical and his temper had started to flare at the slightest provocation. That's when he'd decided it was time for a break.

He'd put in for a leave of absence, not knowing what he'd do for six months, but at that point not really caring. When the chief asked him if he might want to take on an assignment helping out an old friend of his, it almost seemed like the offer had been "heaven-sent."

Of course, Crow didn't believe in heaven. And Sal used to, but he wasn't so sure even he did anymore.

Regardless, here he was, in the home of Sara Michaels, a rising star on the Christian music scene, wondering if he'd lost his mind. He'd spent four years surrounded by drug addicts and hardened criminals. Now he'd be guarding a twenty-five-year-old woman the critics said had a voice like an "angel," while trying to find out who was so determined to bring her down to earth.

Her manager, a nice woman with a lot of street smarts, had insisted up one side and down the other that her client had nothing to hide. But Crow wasn't convinced. It had been his experience that where there was smoke, there was usually fire.

Actually the investigation was the part that Crow liked best about being a cop—trying to find all the parts to the puzzle and put them together until it all made sense.

Barely perceptible footsteps sounded on the

wooden floor. Instantly alert, Crow rose, his whole attention focused on the sound.

Meg rounded the corner and stopped short at his intense expression, her eyes widening in surprise. "Hold your fire. I come in peace."

"Looks like you made it out alive," he said. Meg had told him she wanted to talk to her client in private first. He had his own reservations about playing the role of Sara Michaels's boyfriend, but on the other hand it might be a nice change from the hyped-up junkie types he'd been portraying for the past several years. "How'd it go?"

"It's a no-go on the boyfriend thing. So you don't have to make an appointment with the barber." She smiled brightly. "Not yet anyway."

Crow thought about telling her that cutting his shoulder-length hair had never been an option. It had taken him too long to grow it out. And, though he hadn't yet decided if he was going to return to the narcotics unit once his leave was up, he'd always been a firm believer in keeping his options open. But it was a moot point now. "How are you going to explain my presence then?"

It didn't matter to him, but it had seemed to be a big concern of hers. When he'd met with her and the chief yesterday, he must have heard the words *adverse publicity* a hundred times. That's why she'd initially come up with the boyfriend cover story.

"Sara agreed some protection might be warranted," Meg said quickly. "I think if anyone asks, we should just say it's a precaution in light of what happened to that country singer last month."

"Okay by me," Crow said.

"One more thing." Meg's gaze met his. "She thinks that you're just some bodyguard I hired."

He hesitated, measuring her for a moment. "What are you saying?"

"Sara is adamant about not having a P.I. or cop involved. So I think, for now, it would be best to keep the fact that I've hired you to do some investigation just between the two of us."

"I don't like it." Crow narrowed his gaze. "I need her cooperation to make this work."

"It may be a little more difficult," Meg conceded. "But I'm sure you've faced many difficult situations in your years on the force and prevailed."

"Maybe." Crow wondered what the woman had against cops. She had to be hiding something. But what could it be? In preparation for this assignment, Crow had pored over dozens of articles. The singer had a squeaky-clean image.

For now anyway.

Someone obviously knew something that could turn this young woman's life upside down. Had she dabbled in drugs and sex? Maybe even had some brushes with the law?

His initial run on her hadn't turned up anything but whatever her secret was, he'd discover it. Whether she wanted him to or not.

"Here he is." The door swung open and Meg entered the room with a large dark-haired mountain of a man at her side. "He's perfect, don't you think?"

Sara's mouth went dry and her heart picked up speed. It took all her strength to pull her gaze from his.

Perfect?

Sara had always used that word to describe James—James, who was tall, blond and beautiful. With compelling gray eyes, firm features and a confident set of his shoulders, her publicist garnered admiring glances wherever they went. His hair was always cut in the latest style and his clothing choices complemented his conservative nature. Thanks to regular workouts in a local gym, James's body was well toned but not overly muscular.

But the man before her was anything but perfect. He looked like a refugee from a Harley-Davidson rally, with his burgundy T-shirt, hair past his shoulders and a barbed-wire tattoo encircling his right bicep. Standing at least six foot two, he may have been the same height as James, but he dwarfed the man in build. Crow's chest was broad and his jeans molded against a pair of muscular thighs. If he wasn't a bodybuilder, he should have been.

Sara lifted her gaze and found him staring. Amusement flickered in his eyes and she knew he'd seen where her gaze had been focused.

She shifted her attention to his arm. "I've never seen the appeal of tattoos."

He raised one dark brow.

Sara lifted her chin. She'd seen his type before…lived with his type before. "What can I say? I don't like tattoos."

And I don't like you.

"Don't get one, then," he said with a careless shrug.

And Meg wanted this man to stay?

"Meg, why don't you show Mr.…?" Sara waved her hand as if his name was too inconsequential to remember.

"Crow," he volunteered, that infuriating self-satisfied smile still lingering on his lips.

"Mr. Crow around the place." Sara slanted a sideways glance at James. Through all this he'd remained silent. But he didn't need to say a word. The look of disapproval on his face said it all. "James and I are going out to dinner. We can talk about this bodyguard thing when—"

"For starters," Crow interrupted. "From now on, where you go, I go."

"I don't think—"

"It'll take me only a few minutes to settle in. My suitcase is in the hall. If you'll show me to your bedroom..."

"My bedroom?" Sara sat up straight in the chair. "Why in the world would you need to see my bedroom?"

Crow heaved an exasperated sigh. "Because that's where I'll be sleeping."

Chapter Two

"**W**ith me?" Sara's blue eyes flashed.

"No, right outside your door." Crow paused and regarded her thoughtfully. "Disappointed?"

Her eyebrow raised in amused contempt. "Hardly."

Crow smiled to himself. Perhaps he'd been too quick to dismiss the singer as just another pretty face. It seemed she had spunk. This assignment might be more fun than he'd first thought.

"If I'm not with you, how can I protect you?" he said in a reasonable tone.

"Give me a break." She scoffed. "Next thing I know, you'll be reminding me of that scene from *Psycho* and I'll find you in my shower. All in the name of 'protecting me,' of course."

An image of woman and steam flashed through

his mind. Crow grinned. "Every job has its draw-backs."

"I didn't think a man like you would consider that a drawback."

"Sara." James's voice was low and smooth but filled with command. "I think this discussion has gone far enough."

A hint of irritation tightened Sara's lips. She hated it when James treated her like a child. "Lighten up, James. We were only kidding."

Meg stifled a chuckle.

"I'm not kidding." Crow shifted his gaze to Sara. "I've given Meg my word I'll do whatever it takes to keep you safe. And if that means being with you 24/7, that's what it will be."

What was it with these men? Sara squared her shoulders. "I can take care of myself."

"Not against a stalker." He shook his head. Though he admired her courage, if she didn't start taking this seriously, she could end up being hurt. Or worse. "Not alone."

"I won't be alone." She flashed Mr. *GQ* at her side a smile. "James can stay with me. He can protect me."

Crow stared at the man, with his perfectly creased slacks and freshly starched shirt. He'd seen the type before. Worked out faithfully in the gym three times a week, but didn't know what it meant to fight for your life. In his estimation, Sara would be better off with Fifi, his grandmother's arthritic poodle, for protection.

Crow started to smile, then stopped. This was no joke.

"Just because he's your lover doesn't mean he can protect you." Experience made him speak harsher than he'd intended. "Can he handle a gun? Does he know how to fight?" Crow shifted his gaze from Sara to James.

"For your information, Sara and I are *not* lovers." James shot Sara a chastising look. "Neither one of us believes in premarital intimacy, so I'm sure she didn't mean to give you that impression."

For a second, Crow couldn't figure out what the man was babbling about. Premarital intimacy? He'd asked if he knew how to use a gun and the guy wanted to give him his sexual history?

"I don't care if you've had premarital intimacy with her," Crow said. "I'm asking if you can protect her."

"If I had to, I could." James said, his eyes ice cold. "But I firmly believe that most disagreements can be resolved with words. And prayer. Physical violence is rarely needed."

Crow waited for the man to laugh. When he didn't, he realized with a twinge of horror that James was serious.

"Talk and prayer? Man, you obviously didn't

have any brothers." Crow didn't bother phrasing it as a question. He already knew the answer.

"I have two older sisters," James snapped, his carefully held control starting to unravel. "What does that have to do with anything?"

"Forget it." Crow thought of Tony and Nick. Talk and prayer? It would have never worked with those two. He'd have been six feet under before he was ten.

"I suppose *you* have brothers," Sara said.

"Two." He ignored her sarcasm. "If I didn't know how to fight back then, I wouldn't be standing here today."

"Sounds like my childhood," Sara said, surprising him with a wry grin.

James's eyes narrowed.

"What do these brothers of yours do now?" James's polite tone didn't fool Crow in the least.

"They work," he said. Crow hated talking about his family, but not because he was ashamed of them. On the contrary, he was proud of their success. But he'd never been one to brag, and talking about his brothers always sounded too much like bragging. Tony had already made partner in a well-known St. Louis law firm and Nick was an orthopedic surgeon with a thriving practice.

"They work," James repeated, putting one finger to his lips as if pondering Crow's words. "It's unfortunate, isn't it, that being able to punch out another guy doesn't always translate into a successful career when we grow up."

"Let it go, James." Meg, who'd remained silent up to this point, cast him a pointed glance.

"If he's ashamed…"

"The oldest is a doctor. The youngest is an attorney," Crow said, meeting the other man's gaze before shifting his attention to Sara. "And they're both great guys."

Because Crow was looking at Sara, he could see the surprise flicker across her face. He didn't have to look at Meg or James to know the question that was in her eyes was in theirs, as well.

"I'm sure your parents are proud…of them," James said grudgingly. "Two out of three isn't bad. At least if you get low on money, they could probably bail you out."

Crow resisted the urge to belt the guy, and after that, to slap himself up the side of the head. Why had he ever taken this job? After all, this was supposed to be his time to recharge, to get back to being Sal Tucci: the guy who used to love going to church with his family, playing football with the nieces and nephews on the back lawn and hanging out with his friends. Sometimes he wondered if he'd ever be that man again.

"Crow—" Meg touched his arm "—let me take you upstairs and show you where you'll be sleeping."

"Where are you putting him?" Sara said.

"Wherever I think works best," Crow said pointedly.

Meg ignored them both.

"I think the nursery would be ideal." Meg's eyes twinkled. "The sofa in there pulls out into a bed."

"Nursery?" Crow slanted a questioning gaze at Sara. "You got a kid?"

"Of course not!"

"Oh, Crow." Meg laughed. "I told you Sara's not married."

"I know lots of women who have kids and they've never been married."

"I bet you do," James said. "But Sara's not like the women you know."

Crow clenched his jaw. The guy was really starting to get on his nerves.

"When this house was built, the owners had a nursery adjoin the master suite," Meg said, obviously deciding the best way to deal with the tension was to ignore it.

"I'm not sure I like the idea of him sleeping there." Sara's gaze was troubled.

"It's either that or your bed, sweetheart." Crow could almost hear his mother's sharp reproach. She'd been a stickler about her boys treating women with respect. He shoved the memory aside.

She'd taught *Sal* those lessons. This was *Crow's* assignment. "Either is fine with me."

"I don't like the idea." James frowned. "People will start talking. We don't need any kind of adverse—"

"I think you're making way too much of this, James," Meg interrupted. "Annie's doing all the cooking and cleaning this summer and she's as loyal as they come. As far as everyone else is concerned, Crow is a bodyguard and an old friend of Sara's."

"Sara doesn't have any friends with long hair." James cast a derisive look at Crow.

Crow's lips turned up in a smile. "She does now."

Dinner had gone better than Sara had hoped, even though Crow had insisted on coming along and James had maintained a stony silence through the first half of the meal.

After dessert, Crow excused himself to make a phone call and Sara waited until he'd left the room before she turned to James. "What do you think?"

"He has excellent table manners." James dabbed the corners of his lips with the napkin. "That surprised me."

"I'm not talking about knowing which fork to use." Sara leaned across the table and lowered her voice. "What do you think about this bodyguard thing? Doesn't it seem a bit of an overkill?"

James paused thoughtfully. "Actually that incident in Nashville last month has everyone on edge. I guess I wouldn't be surprised to see more performers hiring them."

"You're saying you approve?" If he'd told her he and Crow had suddenly become best friends, she couldn't have been more surprised. At the very least, Sara had thought James would agree Crow had to go.

"'Approve' might be a bit strong." James took a sip of his decaffeinated coffee. "*Understand* might be a more appropriate word choice."

"I can't believe you're in favor of me living with the guy."

"Keep your voice down," James admonished, casting a quick glance around the half-empty restaurant to see if anyone might have overheard. His features suddenly softened. "I hate the idea of him living in your house. Frankly, I worry about his influence on you."

"His influence?" Her voice was deadly still. Surely James wasn't intimating what she thought.

"Could you please pass me the cream?"

She resisted the urge to give him the cream right in his face, opting instead to hand it to him and wait while he measured precisely one teaspoon of cream and stirred it into his coffee.

"James." Sara kept her tone even. "What did you mean you worry about his influence on me?"

James took a long sip of coffee and shifted uncomfortably in his chair. "Forget I said anything."

"Tell me." Her gaze pinned his.

"Sara…"

She waited.

"Okay, but you're not going to like it." James heaved a resigned sigh. He sat forward and folded his hands in front of him on the table as if praying for heavenly intervention. Sara suspected the way this conversation was headed he was going to need it. "The guy's got that—for want of a better word—animal magnetism, that a certain type of woman could find hard to resist."

Sara's blood ran cold. "A certain type of woman."

"I'm not saying this very well." James took a hurried sip of coffee. "Take your mother for example."

A knot formed in the pit of her stomach and she regretted for the hundredth time telling James about her mother. Granted, she hadn't told him everything about those awful years, but she'd told him enough. Enough that he obviously felt free to make snap judgments.

Like mother, like daughter.

"What about my mother?"

"You told me how much she liked long-haired biker guys."

"Yes, and I believe I also said how much *I* despised that type of man." Sara fumbled with her napkin.

James covered her hand with his. "I didn't mean to upset you."

"Lover's quarrel?" Crow pulled out a chair and took his seat opposite Sara. His lips curved up in a grin. "Anything I can do to help?"

James tried to pull his hand back, but deliberately Sara laced her fingers with his and held on.

"We were just getting to the kiss-and-make-up stage," Sara said. "Want to watch?"

"Sara!" A red flush shot up James's neck.

Crow laughed out loud. "Sure, why not?"

Sara grinned and glanced at James. "On second thought, it'll have to be later. James's not much for PDA."

Crow raised a brow. "PDA?"

"Public display of affection." James jerked his hand free of Sara's. "And she's right. I'm not in favor of it. Not at all."

James was mad.

Good.

That comment about her mother had stung. She was nothing like her mother and James knew it. And as far as Crow was concerned, although James was right that Crow did have that certain something, he was wrong about her being susceptible to his charms.

The ride home seemed to take hours. As soon as the car stopped, James mouthed some excuse about stacks of correspondence on his desk and declined Sara's offer to come inside. Almost as an afterthought, he brushed his lips against hers before saying goodbye and driving away.

"I'm glad I didn't stay up just for that." An amused smile hovered on Crow's lips. "I would have had to ask for my money back."

"What money?" Sara unlocked the front door and automatically motioned him inside.

Crow ignored the question and followed her into the hall. "I bet he kisses like a fish."

She whirled, and the gleam in his eyes made Sara wish she'd said good-night the minute she'd walked through the door. Despite knowing she should cut her losses and not encourage him further, Sara couldn't resist having the last word. "I'll have you know James is more than adequate in the kissing department."

His lips twitched.

"He is," she insisted.

"Either you haven't kissed very many men..." He paused and his gaze turned sharp and assessing. She wondered if he'd laugh if he knew James was the *only* man she'd ever kissed. "Or you have extremely low expectations."

"I suppose you think you could do better." The words were out and hanging in the air between them before she could stop them.

His gaze lowered to her lips. "I don't think. I *know* I could."

Sara's mouth went dry and her heart raced.

Crow moved across the room until he stood in front of her, so close she could smell the intoxicating scent of his cologne, so close she could see his eyes weren't black but brown with flecks of hazel, so close if she moved one step forward she'd be in his arms.

"Arrogance is a sin," she said softly.

"I'm not arrogant." He brushed back a strand of her hair with one finger and leaned forward. "I'm confident."

His lips brushed her cheek on their slow journey to her mouth. It was now or never. All she had to do was step back or say no.

But his breath was warm against her face, and on second thought, what would one little kiss hurt? It wouldn't lead to anything else. If he was confident of his ability to kiss, she was confident it wouldn't affect her. So what would be the harm?

She turned slightly, and her arms rose and encircled his neck, her fingers weaving through his soft curls.

Crow's hands spanned her waist and he ran his palms up her sides.

Blood surged from her fingertips to her toes. She couldn't wait any longer. Impulsively she kissed him lightly on the mouth.

He kissed the tip of her nose.

Her skin prickled pleasurably. She breathed a satisfied sigh. "That was very nice."

He smiled and his eyes danced like bubbling chocolate. "That was just the preview."

"Preview?"

"Of what's to come."

Without warning his mouth descended once again. His lips were more persuasive than she cared to admit, and she was shocked at her own eager response.

In the end it took all her strength to step from his arms. All her strength to flash him a nonchalant smile. And most of all, all her strength to walk away and act like the kiss hadn't affected her at all.

Chapter Three

Sara rolled over and hit the snooze button, hoping to delay the inevitable for a few more minutes. But sleep eluded her and she finally had no choice but to open her eyes.

She lifted her lids slowly, knowing with the light would come the memories of last night. Her cheeks warmed at the thought of her wanton behavior.

What had possessed her to kiss Crow? She searched her brain for a plausible excuse. Had she been tired? Stressed? Insane?

But who was she kidding? Deep down she already knew the reason. She'd kissed him because she was attracted to him.

A knot formed in the pit of her stomach. She threw back the quilt and swung her legs over the side of the bed.

Attracted? To Crow?

Ridiculous.

Sara banished the crazy thought and sprang to her feet. She'd get dressed and then she'd think. She headed into the bathroom and rummaged through the drawer for her brush. She pulled it through her tangled blond hair with savage jerks, almost relishing the pain.

She couldn't be attracted to someone like him. She simply couldn't.

Gripping the sides of the sink, she took a deep breath and steadied herself. When she finally looked up into the mirror, she barely recognized the pathetic creature staring back at her.

The image was certainly a far cry from the confident young woman who'd stood on stage just a few months ago and accepted the Sheldon Award as New Artist of the Year.

Sara made a face. She'd kissed the guy. Big deal.

She wouldn't do it again, that much was certain. Although… Her fingers rose to her lips and she couldn't help but remember the warm sweetness of his kiss and how it had left her longing for more.

Don't date a man you wouldn't want to marry.

Meg's motherly advice popped into her head. Although Sara wasn't dating Crow, wouldn't ever date Crow, Meg's sage wisdom could be applied to kissing, as well.

Sara knew the type of man she wanted to marry. She wanted a man who was solid and dependable and a strong Christian. And if the guy was good-looking like James, so much the better.

Men like Crow with their tattoos, long hair and fiery kisses might be exciting, but they were nothing but trouble. Sara's heart lifted. She comforted herself with the knowledge that the kiss with Crow was just a momentary lapse in judgment.

She quickly showered and dressed, pulling on a pair of khaki pants and a blue checked button-down shirt, that James always said made her eyes look more violet than blue. She headed down the stairs to breakfast. The door to the kitchen was partially ajar and Sara pushed it all the way open before she stopped abruptly.

Crow sat at the table like he owned the place, a mug of coffee in one hand, the morning paper in the other.

He glanced up briefly, his gaze shifting pointedly to the clock. "The day's half-gone."

Sara bristled not so much because she felt guilty over sleeping late, but because for some reason the mere sight of him irritated her. "It's only ten-thirty."

"I've been up since seven." Crow dropped one section of the paper onto the table and picked up another.

Sara grabbed a sweet roll from a platter on the

counter and poured herself a cup of coffee. "Seven? Wow, I'm impressed."

His only answer was an unintelligible grumble.

Sara smiled in satisfaction and took a seat at the table opposite him. "Did Meg call?"

Crow briefly tore his gaze from the paper's front page. "She called around eight. I told her you were still alive. She'll be over later."

Sara reached for the sugar and added a couple of teaspoonfuls to her coffee. She stirred it slowly, studying him from under her lashes. Who was this man who had unceremoniously invaded her world?

His ebony hair gleamed in the artificial light. It hung in loose waves past his shoulders. His tanned face was clean shaven and the hint of a spicy aftershave hung in the air between them. With his square jaw and ruggedly chiseled face, Sara was certain if he cut that hair and lost the scowl, he'd be magnificent.

She squinted, trying to visualize him with short hair.

He glanced up and his brows drew together. "Is something wrong?"

She took a bite of the Danish and ignored the warmth rising up her neck. "Why do you ask?"

"For a moment I thought you were giving me the evil eye."

Sara choked on a raisin. She took a sip of coffee to wash it down and used the time to think of a response that made some sense. "I was just trying to see what had you so engrossed."

"It's just a stupid article talking about Johnny Baker's chances of making parole." Crow shook his head in disgust. He folded the paper and handed it to her. "Take it. I've read enough."

"Johnny Baker?" Sara paused, trying to place the name. "Wasn't he that big drug dealer that went to prison a few years back?"

"That's him." Crow's lips tightened.

"But I thought he got ten years." Sara remembered the case now.

"He did. But he's served enough time to be eligible for parole. And according to the papers, he's a 'changed' man. He's discovered the Lord." Crow snorted. "Yeah, right."

Sara added more sugar to her coffee but kept her gaze focused on the newsprint. "You don't think a person can change?"

"No way."

Surprised at the vehemence of his response, Sara glanced up and found his gaze riveted on her. She shifted uncomfortably. It almost seemed as if he could see straight through to her soul.

"The thief on the cross repented," Sara said. "And Christ forgave him."

"I just know what I've seen." Crow's tone was flat. "And believe me, I haven't seen too many people who have really changed. Once a drug dealer, always a drug dealer. Once a thief, always a thief.''

Sara's breath caught in her throat. ''You can't believe that.''

''You can't believe that finding God and saying you're sorry is all that it takes.''

That's exactly what I believe.

Sara shrugged. ''It doesn't matter what I believe. I can tell I'm not going to change your mind.''

''You've got that right.'' Crow's gaze flicked over her. ''I know what's true and there isn't anyone who's going to convince me different.''

''Whatever.'' Someday she hoped someone would help Crow discover what God's grace was all about. But that someone wouldn't be her. ''Could you hand me the entertainment section? I want to see if they've reviewed my latest CD.''

''Your career's pretty hot right now, isn't it?''

''I guess.'' Sara opened the paper and flipped the pages.

''According to your manager, those threatening notes started coming right after you won that award.''

''They weren't threatening,'' Sara said.

''Whatever,'' he said, mimicking the word she'd used earlier.

She smiled.

''It's not funny.'' Crow's face took on a familiar

scowl. "Jealousy can make people do strange things."

He was so far off the mark, she wanted to laugh. But she decided to humor him instead. "So you're thinking this note writer is another performer?"

"Could be," Crow said. "Anybody you can think of that would like to see your career take a nosedive?"

"Not a one." Her fellow performers were incapable of such actions.

"There's got to be one or two that—"

"There's not," Sara said emphatically. "Why are you so curious anyway?"

"Don't you want to find out who's responsible for the notes?"

She noticed he didn't answer her question, but she let it go. "Like I told Meg, it's probably just some kind of joke. And frankly I'm sick to death of thinking *and* talking about it."

"What do you want to talk about then?"

Sara leaned forward and rested her elbows on the table. She pasted an expectant look on her face. "Why don't you tell me about yourself? I'm dying to know everything about you."

He groaned.

Sara smiled.

"May I help you, sir?"

Crow's gaze flicked briefly to the salesclerk before returning to where Sara stood, flipping through a pile of lingerie. The sign overhead proclaimed Fifty Percent Off And More.

"No, thanks." Crow jerked his head in the direction of the sale table. "I'm just waiting for a friend."

"I understand completely." The man's voice held a hint of amusement and for a brief moment they shared a bond.

Women.

If Crow didn't know better, he'd swear she'd deliberately invented this shopping trip to either get back at him for refusing to tell her anything about himself or to drive him crazy. And it was working. In the past two hours they'd been in five stores. She'd worked her way through countless racks and tables. And he'd been there, guarding her body.

His smile widened. Even though her clothes did nothing to accentuate her figure, it didn't take a rocket scientist to see her curves were definitely in all the right places and, even though at five feet five she wasn't as tall as he liked...

As tall as he liked?

Crow brought himself up short. She was his client. When the assignment was over, he'd probably go back to the police force and to his first and only love: his job.

A man he'd never seen before pushed his way

through the crowd and stood beside Sara. Crow's eyes narrowed. He quickly covered the distance between them but the guy in the navy suit had vanished as quickly as he had appeared.

"Where did he go?"

Sara dropped the lingerie she'd been holding back on the table. "What are you talking about?"

"The man in the suit," he said impatiently, his gaze searching the nearby aisles. "You were just talking to him."

"Oh, you mean Ralph." Sara smiled. "He works in Menswear on the weekends."

"What did he want?" Crow snapped.

Normally females quivered when he let his impatience show. Sara didn't bat an eye.

"If you must know, he wanted to meet me." Her smile widened. "His thirteen-year-old daughter is a big fan of mine."

"Why didn't you tell me that in the first place?"

"Because you didn't say 'pretty please.'" A dimple he'd never noticed before flashed in one cheek. "You're certainly grouchy. Not interested in women's lingerie?"

"Oh, I'm very interested in women's lingerie," he said. "Taking it off that is." Crow forgot for the moment he wasn't talking to one of the guys.

To his surprise, she laughed. "I should have known better than to ask."

"Are you hungry?" Crow said, changing the subject. "I know a great place not far from here."

"Don't tell me." She crossed her arms and studied him, an impish grin on her face. "They serve great brats and beer?"

"No, that place is way across town." He cupped her elbow in his hand. "Trust me. You'll like this one."

"Do I have a choice?"

Crow didn't answer. He was too busy hustling her out of the mall and hoping that after she filled up on pasta and bread, she'd be too tired to shop anymore.

The Grotto had been a favorite of his family when he'd been growing up. It had been years since he'd been back but he'd heard that it still had the best spaghetti carbonara in the city.

Since it was after one, the lunch crowd had thinned and Sara and Crow were seated immediately.

"In the winter I'd kill for this table." Sara gestured to the huge stone fireplace next to them. "It figures the only time I'd get it would be in the summer."

"Don't just sit and complain." He shoved the menu at her, irritated that she hadn't instantly fallen in love with the place. "See what you want."

"When you put it so nicely, how can I refuse?"

She picked up the menu and shot him a smile they both knew wasn't sincere. "Do you think you growl so much because all that hair makes you feel like a bear?"

"I do not—" The words stopped in his throat at the sight of a slender dark-haired woman being escorted to a table on the other side of the dining room.

He shoved his chair back and stood abruptly. "I'll be right back."

How long had it been since he'd seen her? Six months? It had to be longer than that. She'd been in Paris for almost a year, and the one time she'd made it home, he'd been undercover eating cold pizza in a dingy motel room.

Crow came up silently from behind and tapped her on the shoulder. He lowered his voice to a husky rumble. "What do you think you're doing?"

She whirled around. "Sal."

Joy lit her face and she sprung to her feet, enveloping him in a massive hug. "It's been so long."

"Too long." He hugged her back. They'd fought like cats and dogs when they were younger, but he had missed her. "When did you get back?"

"Two weeks ago. I've tried to call you several times but no one answered. Let me look at you." She stepped back and surveyed him at arm's length. "What's with the hair? It looks even longer than before."

He chuckled. Raven had never made a secret of the fact she preferred his hair short.

"I'll get it cut. One of these days."

"I could do it now." Her dark eyes gleamed with mischief. "If you remember, the knives here are razor sharp."

He was tempted to say "Go ahead and do it," but she was just the type to call his bluff. His lips curved up in an indulgent smile.

"I'm busy now," Crow said. "Some other time."

Raven reached over and fingered a lock of his hair. "It would only take a second."

Crow laughed and captured her hand with his, giving it a squeeze before releasing it.

"C'mon, Sal—" Raven stopped suddenly. She lowered her voice. "Or are you Crow?"

The name sounded funny coming from her, even though she'd been the one to suggest it when he was looking for a street name all those years ago.

Raven had said it was sweet justice for all the teasing she'd taken as a child for her given name. In their family the boys had been named by his father and had been given fine Italian names: Anthony, Nicholas and Salvadore. When his mother finally had her girl, his father said she went crazy. How else could you explain a woman naming her only daughter after her favorite soap opera character?

"Crow," he said. "But this is a special situation."

"Is the blonde a cop, too?"

"Sara?" Crow smiled. "Hardly. But how'd you know I was with her?"

"Because, dear brother—" Raven leaned closer and whispered against his ear "—she's been shooting daggers ever since you put your arms around me."

"You're letting your imagination run wild." Crow chuckled. "Sara doesn't like men with long hair. Or tattoos."

"I like her already. Even if she is wrong about you." Raven brushed a kiss across his cheek and several men at a nearby table cast admiring glances her way.

He didn't blame them. Even if she was his sister, she was undeniably lovely, with thick black hair and piercing gold-flecked brown eyes.

"Are you going to introduce me?" Her eyes sparkled.

"No."

"C'mon, Sal…"

He groaned.

She flashed him an apologetic smile. "Okay, *Crow*. Since I got back from Paris, my life has been incredibly dull."

"Call up Nick or Tony."

"What, and hear about the latest advances in back surgery? Or some new legal precedent? No way. Don't get me wrong. I love 'em to death, but their lives aren't nearly as exciting as yours."

He shook his head, steeling himself against her imploring look.

"Okay, I'll introduce myself."

She was halfway across the room before he caught up with her.

"Raven, listen to me…"

She arched one dark brow and met his gaze with a determined look of her own.

He heaved a resigned sigh. "Okay, but she doesn't know anything about Sal Tucci and she doesn't know I'm a cop. She thinks I'm just some bodyguard she hired."

"What's going on? Why does she need a body-guard?"

He narrowed his gaze.

"Oh, all right, keep your little secrets." She eyed him calculatingly. "Are you going to tell her who I am?"

"Get serious. If I don't want her to know who I am, why would I let her know you're my sister?" He couldn't keep the disgust from his voice.

"Good point." She nodded thoughtfully. "So, if I'm not your sister, then I'm your…?"

"Old friend."

"Gotcha." A mischievous smile lifted her lips. "I think this is going to be great fun."

Great fun?

Crow groaned. It was going to be a disaster.

Chapter Four

Sara took a sip of her water and with unabashed interest studied the woman talking to Crow. From the tips of her strappy leather sandals to the diamond studs twinkling in her ears, the dark-haired beauty exemplified good taste and class.

Whatever type of female Sara had thought would be Crow's type, it wasn't someone like this. The two were obviously more than good friends. The flash of joy in his eyes when he'd first seen her and the hug she'd given him told Sara that much.

Her gaze slid to the woman's left hand. She breathed a sigh of relief at the sight of the bare finger. Of course, it didn't matter to her if Crow was married or not. But Sara prided herself on her intuition, and her intuition said that a marriage between these two would be a disaster.

A smile lifted her lips at the thought of Crow mingling at a country club party or teeing off at a golf outing.

"Sara?"

Her head jerked up and her cheeks warmed. While she'd been lost in her foolish imaginings, Crow and the woman had crossed the room and now stood before her.

"You're back." Instinctively Sara widened her smile.

"I'd like you to meet Raven. She's my..." His voice faltered for a second. "She's an old friend of mine."

Granted, Sara didn't know Crow very well, but even she didn't miss his hesitation.

Sara paused. The name was obviously a fake. An old friend? She narrowed her gaze. Did Crow think she was stupid?

"Nice to meet you...Raven?" Sara put extra emphasis on the name and raised a questioning brow, but the woman just smiled.

"And Raven, this is—"

"Robin." Sara extended her hand.

"Robin?" Crow frowned. "That's not your name."

"I didn't think it mattered." Sara shrugged.

"I'd venture a guess that Crow isn't your real name and Raven isn't hers, so I picked my own."

Crow's frown deepened.

"She's clever, Crow. I like her." Raven laughed throatily. "However, I have to admit that Raven *is* my given name."

"Really?" Sara searched the woman's hazel eyes. If there was anything she hated, it was being played for a fool. But there was no hint of deception in the direct gaze.

"It's the truth. I swear to God." Raven laughed again and Sara found herself warming to the woman.

"Okay, I believe you." Sara shifted her gaze to Crow. "But don't even try to tell me Crow is *your* real name."

He exchanged a glance with Raven before answering. "It may not have come from my mother, but it has been my name for more years than I care to remember."

Sara studied him for a long moment.

"Would you like something to drink?" The waiter who'd been standing off to the side casting admiring glances at Raven took advantage of the break in conversation.

"Won't you join us?" Sara put aside the name issue and gestured to a chair. Lunching with Raven could be interesting. There was no telling what little tidbits about Crow the woman might let slip.

The same thought must have crossed Crow's mind because the look he shot Raven was anything but inviting.

Raven shook her head regretfully. "I'd love to, I really would. But I'm meeting a friend for lunch."

Her eyes narrowed and she waved across the room at a thin blond woman with wire-rimmed glasses. "In fact, there she is now. I've got to run."

They said quick goodbyes, but Sara noticed that Raven still took a moment to give Crow another hug before she left.

His gaze followed her across the room before he took his seat opposite Sara.

"She seems nice." Sara smoothed the linen napkin on her lap. "You said she's an old friend?"

"Known her forever," Crow said, taking a hard roll from the basket before handing it to her. "But that's a long story. I'd rather talk about you. Tell me, how'd you get started in the music business anyway?"

Sara took a bread stick, broke it in half and chewed thoughtfully, buying some time. She didn't want to talk about *her* past.

Although she'd told her story to the tabloids and magazines often enough, she still hesitated to tell it to him. All these years she'd been able to gloss over some events and leave others out entirely.

"Sara?" Crow pressed. "How did you get started?"

She suspected Crow would keep at her until he got all the details. But he wouldn't get *all* the details. She'd see to that.

Sara lifted her chin. She had her secrets and that's what they'd stay.

Her secrets.

Her past.

God had forgiven her. Maybe one day she'd forgive herself.

Crow had never been a patient man. When he asked a question, he expected an immediate answer. Normally people complied.

Whether it was because of what others told him was a menacing scowl or an intimidating manner, he didn't know. But most knew better than to mess with him.

Only a few had openly defied him. And he could count those on one hand: his mother, his sister and his old partner on the force, Angel Weston. But now Sara seemed inclined to resist answering one simple question. Could he be losing his touch? Getting soft?

His frown deepened. "I asked—"

"—how I got started. I know," Sara said with a resigned sigh. "Believe me, it's not that interesting. I mean I didn't wait tables for years struggling to make ends meet. It just all sort of fell into place. It's really quite boring.''

"Start at the beginning.'' Crow waved aside her protests. "I want to know everything.''

But Sara didn't start at the beginning. Instead she began when she was sixteen, in foster care and "utterly miserable.''

"I didn't do much except go to school, come home and listen to CDs.'' She brushed back a strand of honey-colored hair with the tips of her fingers. "Then one day, in a weak moment, I agreed to go to a church picnic with my foster parents.''

"A weak moment?'' Crow raised a brow.

Sara chuckled. "That was my thought at the time. Up to then I'd resisted all their invitations to be involved in church activities. But that day I was bored out of my mind and decided it would be better than doing nothing.''

"What happened?''

"I had fun.'' The smile lit up her face. "The kids were warm and accepting and, crazy as it sounds, I felt like I was home.''

He could picture the scene. His parents were both active in the church and he'd been heavily involved in church functions his whole life. That is, until he'd gone undercover and assumed the identity of Crow.

Crow who couldn't—who wouldn't—be caught

dead in a church. Over time his newfound cynicism had battered against the teachings of his youth. And his faith had floundered. "I used to feel that way."

"Used to?" A curious glint filled her gaze.

He cursed himself. They were discussing her life, not his. Crow ignored the question and attempted to steer the conversation back to her past. "What happened after the picnic? You had a good time and then...?"

"I started going to church, joined the choir—and the rest is history."

Like a neat and tidy bundle, she'd tied up the past in a single sentence. But Crow knew there had to be more to it than that. "Tell me about the choir."

Though he saw she hid it well, Crow could tell she was irritated by his questions.

"We had a great group of singers and it wasn't long before we started getting a lot of recognition. Our choir director, Mr. Marcus, believed we witnessed every time we sang and so he rarely said no when someone asked us to perform."

"And?" Crow tried to follow her lead and not let his impatience show. But she was wearing him down by making him fish for every detail.

"At one of the events I had a solo. A music producer heard me and—"

"The rest is history?"

She smiled. "Exactly."

"How old were you?"

"When?" Sara took a long sip of iced tea and gazed up at him innocently through lowered lashes.

He was sure of it now. The woman was trying to drive him stark raving mad. He heaved an exasperated sigh. "When you got your record deal."

"Twenty-one." Sara leaned back in her chair.

He waited for her to elaborate.

She remained silent.

"You said you were sixteen when you joined the choir. What happened between sixteen and twenty-one?"

"Nothing much." Sara crumbled the last of her bread stick into little pieces on her plate and shrugged. "I graduated from high school. Then I went to Washington University and got a degree in Music and Performing Arts."

Though she downplayed her accomplishments, he couldn't help but be impressed. Washington University had a good reputation. Though the private liberal arts school in St. Louis wasn't tremendously expensive, it certainly cost more than a state-supported college. "That school isn't cheap."

"I was lucky enough to get some grants and scholarships," Sara said simply.

"I thought maybe your parents helped you." Crow said, keeping his gaze fixed in an attempt to gauge her response.

"I never knew my father." Sara's words were so carefully measured, Crow had no doubt he was being given her pat response. "And my mother relinquished me to foster care when I was fifteen."

"Why would she do that?" Crow asked bluntly.

"I think she wanted to give me a better life." Sara kept her gaze down. She took an extraordinary amount of time spooning dressing onto the already-saturated salad.

"Is that what she said?" For a moment he felt as if he was back on the force interrogating a suspect.

Sara looked up and met his gaze unflinchingly. "We never really talked about it."

He could tell it was a lie. She knew exactly why her mother had left. Whatever the reason, it had hurt her then. And it was hurting her now.

Over the years Crow had given his own mother plenty of reasons to throw in the towel, but she'd always stood behind him. And, try as he might, he couldn't imagine that Sara had pulled half the stunts he had.

But he reminded himself, Sara's mother might have left because of other reasons. In his years as a police officer, he'd seen many situations where a single mother had too many children and too little money to care for them. "Do you have any brothers or sisters?"

She shook her head. "Nope, just me."

The excuse of too many mouths to feed vanished.

"Then why did she leave you?"

"I told you I don't know," she snapped. "I never asked."

He was getting somewhere now. Any reaction was better than that cool facade that told him nothing. "Why not?"

If his gaze hadn't been riveted to her face, he might have missed the flash of pain that momentarily clouded her features.

Sara's fingers tightened around her salad fork. "My mother and I haven't spoken in years."

"Really?" Crow took a drink of his tea and ignored the tone in her voice that said the subject was off-limits. "Does she live in the area?"

"Don't ask me." Sara shrugged. "We lost contact years ago."

He took another sourdough roll and studied her carefully. Her nonchalance didn't ring true. "I could help you find her."

"No!" She spoke so loudly, several people at a nearby table turned to stare.

Crow restrained a smile. He'd hit another nerve. After a slow start, this was turning out to be a very productive lunch. But he could tell by her bulldog expression that he'd gone as far as he dared today.

He raised his hands in mock surrender. "Okay, subject closed."

The first chance he got, he'd start doing a little digging. See what he could find out about Sara's past. See what skeletons she might have in her closet. And see if whatever she was hiding might not just be coming back to haunt her.

Chapter Five

I could help you find her.

Despite a long midafternoon bubble bath, Sara's tangled emotions were still as tightly strung as a guitar string. And it didn't help that Crow's offer kept running through her head like a broken record.

Sara tossed a still-damp strand of hair back from her face and rubbed the plum-scented lotion onto her legs with a vengeance. She'd known Crow would be trouble the minute she'd seen him.

Who did he think he was, offering to find her mother? If Sara had wanted to see the woman again, didn't he think she would have done her own search before now?

She slathered the lotion on her shoulders and chest.

Not that she hadn't considered it. Many, many

times in fact. But among other things, the thought of what she'd say once they were face-to-face always stopped her.

The regret that Sara had borne stoically for so many years rose up and threatened to overwhelm her.

Sara swallowed hard. Was she destined to live with the guilt forever? She set the bottle of lotion down on the dressing table.

She should have known better. If she had known the repercussions, she never would have so much as looked at the money. She certainly never would have touched it. And above all she never would have taken it.

Sara sighed. She'd always believed in living in the present and leaving the past where it belonged, in the past.

For the past ten years, she'd successfully done just that. Every time a memory of her former life slipped through and invaded her thoughts, she'd quickly and deliberately shoved it back to the far recesses of her mind where all the sins of her past resided.

Although holidays and her birthday were still difficult, the ache in her heart when she thought of her mother and what had happened lessened with each passing year.

Then the notes started. She'd come back from an exhausting European tour to find the first one waiting. Despite Meg's insistence that taking care of correspondence was part of a manager's duties, Sara had always insisted on handling all her own mail.

Sara remembered opening the envelope as if it was yesterday, instead of three months ago. Even without closing her eyes she could visualize the words and their placement on the plain white paper.

Would your fans still love you if they knew you were a thief?

Thankfully it was the only note she'd received that mentioned the money. The subsequent ones focused on pride and sin and God's punishment.

But it wasn't God's punishment that worried Sara—she knew He'd forgiven her—it was the punishment Gary Burke had in mind. Once she'd read the first note, Sara had known Gary wrote it. She would have given anything if it had been some crazy obsessed fan instead of him. A guy who no doubt blamed her for the time he'd spent in prison. And she knew involving the police would only make matters worse.

Sooner or later Gary would make his demands. Only then would she know what it would cost her to buy his silence.

It wouldn't be cheap or easy. Gary had a mean streak a mile wide. If he could hurt her as well as take her money, she had no doubt he'd do it. After all, she'd experienced his cruelty firsthand.

That's why she'd finally given in to Meg's pressure and agreed to a bodyguard. The memory of what Gary's knuckles could do to soft skin turned her stomach.

An alarm she'd set earlier buzzed noisily from the bedside stand. Sara shut it off and forced her attention to more immediate concerns.

James would be ringing the doorbell in thirty minutes. Punctuality, he often said jokingly, was his middle name, and he wouldn't appreciate being kept waiting.

Tonight they were attending a black-tie cocktail party that James said was essential to her career. Last week he'd managed to snag a copy of the guest list. The names read like a Who's Who of St. Louis. According to James, this would be the perfect opportunity to scout some backers for her next tour.

Wait until he finds out Crow is coming.

Just thinking of James's reaction forced the smile from Sara's lips. Though she hated to stereotype anyone, Sara knew that Crow was anything but a black-tie kind of guy. With his long hair and menacing appearance, he'd probably stick out like a sore thumb.

But Crow had made a good point. What was the

purpose in having a bodyguard if you left him at home?

Surprisingly he hadn't balked when she'd told him he'd have to wear a tux. But he'd laughed when she'd added, "And cut your hair."

She wondered where he'd be able to find a tux at this late hour. He'd seemed confident he could, but she had her doubts.

Her gaze shifted to the gold clock on her dresser and her eyes widened. Instead of worrying about what Crow would be wearing, she needed to be making some decisions herself.

Sara moved quickly to her walk-in closet, flung open the door and stepped inside. Her eyes scanned the long rack on the right that held nothing but party dresses.

Remember when you didn't have even one? When you would have given anything to have a dress for that freshman formal?

Her heart twisted. She remembered all too well.

Sara took a deep breath and forced her attention back to the row of dresses. She reached for the one that she'd bought in Chicago at a cute little place on Michigan Avenue. It was black rayon georgette with a beaded neckline and peasant sleeves.

She pulled it carefully over her head, making sure not to muss her makeup, then moved to stand in front of the full-length mirror.

Her smile widened at the reflection, and she

heaved a sigh of relief. It was even better than she remembered. Simple and elegantly understated, the dress fit her snugly, making her look slender and feminine.

It didn't hurt that she'd gotten a little sun in the last couple of weeks and her skin now glowed with a healthy tan. Her long, thick hair tumbled carelessly down her back in loose waves, the sun streaks blending in with the natural gold color.

Even her change in makeup had worked out. She'd tried a couple of new techniques recommended by the beauty consultant James had suggested. Her eyes now were big and twice as blue and her lashes, full and dark. But it was the lipstick that made the most difference. Her lips looked pouty and extremely kissable.

Sara wondered what Crow—er, James—would say when he saw her dressed fit to kiss—er, kill. She smiled at her reflection and reached for her evening bag.

She couldn't wait to find out.

Chapter Six

"You, in a tux?" Nick Tucci leaned back in his leather chair and laughed out loud. Only ten months apart, the resemblance between the two brothers was striking. If Crow's hair had been cut stylishly short like Nick's, they could have easily passed for twins. "Now I've heard it all."

"Do you have one I can borrow, or not?" Crow glanced at his watch. If Nick didn't have a tux, he didn't have much time left to find another.

A tiny smile played at the corner of his brother's lips as if he was amused by Crow's curtness. Still, Nick didn't hesitate. He turned to his housekeeper who'd entered the room with a fresh carafe of coffee. "Jeannette, would you get my tux from the closet, please?"

Jeannette Post had been with his brother since he'd finished his residency several years before. The silver-haired sixty-something-year-old made her own bread and fussed after him like a doting grandmother. She often laughed that Nick should have lived in the fifties. He wanted nothing more than to find a woman to take care of him and his house. Unfortunately he seemed to pick women who were immersed in their careers and who cringed at the idea of being a ''just a homemaker.''

''Certainly, Dr. Tucci.'' The older woman smiled fondly at her boss. Despite their close relationship, she refused to call him by his given name, insisting it wasn't proper. ''Do you want me to get the shoes, too?''

Nick paused and his eyebrow quirked. ''Size twelve still work for you, Sal?''

''I'm surprised you need to ask,'' Crow said. ''We've worn the same size since we were kids.''

''A lot has changed since then.'' Nick's gaze lingered on his brother.

Disappointment coursed through Crow. ''Tell me, Nick. When did you turn into such a snob?''

''What are you talking about?'' Nick set his cup on the endtable and leaned forward, his eyes flashing. ''I'm not a snob.''

''C'mon, Nick.'' Crow knew he should let the subject drop, but he couldn't. ''Lately, you and

Tony, even Mom and Dad have started to look at me like I'm some kind of lowlife.''

Nick started to protest but Crow impatiently waved him silent. The intensity of his feelings surprised him. He'd been telling himself he was happy the way he was and he didn't care what anyone thought, including his family. Now, suddenly, it was important that Nick understood.

''I'm still the same guy. The long hair and tattoo doesn't change who I am.''

Nick stared at Crow for a long moment. ''But you have changed, Sal. Big-time.''

''Nick, you don't—''

''Let me finish.'' Nick blew a harsh breath. ''We all change. I'm not the same guy I was when I got out of medical school. It's not right or wrong. It's just the way it is. But don't try to tell me that the things you've seen and experienced on the streets haven't changed you, as well.''

Crow took a moment and thought back to all the things he'd seen since he'd made detective: people killed over pocket change, kids strung out on coke, a baby left in a trash can to die…

He pushed the troubling memories aside.

''Maybe you're right,'' Crow admitted grudgingly. But if he had changed, the transformation had happened so gradually, so insidiously, that he hadn't seen it coming. And, even if he had, he knew he couldn't have stopped it.

"But there's something that will never change." Nick took a long sip of coffee. "I'll always be here for you, bro. Remember that. Anytime."

"That goes both ways," Crow said with equal fervor. The two had always been close. Deep down, Crow knew he could count on Nick. Then why couldn't he bring himself to talk to his brother about all the doubts and uncertainties that had plagued him this last year?

Even as he raised the question, Crow knew the answer. How can you ever hope to explain something to someone when you don't understand it yourself?

Knowing Sara was safe with the bodyguard he'd hired for backup, Crow took full advantage of his brother's hospitality. He leisurely showered and dressed at Nick's house. Mrs. Post even stayed late to "see how he cleaned up" and had nodded her approval, saying he was born for black tie. His parents used to say the same thing. Thankfully they were out of town for the weekend or they'd probably be at the party tonight and he'd have to listen to them go on and on about how good he looked.

And he'd have had to admit they would have been right. He *did* look good. But he felt like an impostor in the tux. This was his family's social circle, not his. Not anymore.

Though he'd attended many such functions while growing up—his father had always been a great patron of the arts—once he'd finished the police academy all that had stopped. When Sal became Crow and went undercover, his life had moved in a darker direction, and though he sometimes yearned to go back, he knew he couldn't.

It had been years since he'd attended a cocktail party. The events he'd frequented in the recent past tended to have kegs of beer in one corner and loud music in the other.

At thirty-two, Crow was starting to grow weary of that whole scene. He glanced briefly into the rearview mirror. And of other things, as well.

Last year he'd shaved off the beard. But he'd left the hair untouched.

Tonight when he was rinsing out the shampoo in Nick's shower, Crow couldn't help but think how much easier it would be if his hair were cut short. Because the longer it got, the curlier it became. He'd tried to tame the wild strands by using his brother's blow-dryer, but when that didn't work, he'd given up and pulled it back in a low ponytail.

But tempted though he was to cut it off, it wasn't as simple as a visit to the barber. His career depended on having a certain persona, and the long hair was part of it.

Unfortunately that meant he was going to stick out like a sore thumb tonight. He knew Sara would catch flak for bringing him, if not from James, then from other "well-meaning" friends. Crow could fight his own battles, but he hated to see her get caught in the cross fire.

Why, a tiny voice inside whispered, do you even care?

I'm only doing my job. Looking out for my client is part of that job.

Though the excuse didn't ring completely true, for the moment it satisfied him. He'd go to the party tonight and be the perfect gentleman. But he refused to consider that his personal feelings had anything to do with the actions and the decisions he was making.

She was his client.

He was her bodyguard.

And that's all there was to it.

By the time he pulled up in front of Sara's house and shut off the car, Crow's insides were on fast forward. The place blazed with lights and Crow fumbled for the keys to the front door. Finally finding the one he wanted, he slipped the key into the lock and eased the door open.

"Stop right there," a familiar voice ordered.

"It's only me." Crow raised his hands in mock surrender and grinned at Larry, the backup bodyguard.

"I heard someone at the door." Larry holstered his revolver and a smirk of a smile creased his leathery face. "Now don't you look snazzy. The guys at the gym wouldn't recognize you."

The gym they both frequented had the best boxing facilities in the city, but it also catered to a rather unsavory clientele.

"Yeah, well—" Crow shrugged "—you gotta do what you gotta do."

"I'd trade places with you in a second." The man's beady eyes gleamed. "I bet they'll have tons of booze and you won't have to pay a dime."

"Maybe," Crow said. "But I'll be on duty, remember?"

"Oh, yeah, that's right." The guy lowered his voice. "Guarding the little princess."

Crow hid a grin. Larry called 'em as he saw 'em. He'd told Crow the first time he'd met Sara, with that long blond hair and big blue eyes, she'd reminded him of a princess in one of those storybooks.

"Is she ready?"

Larry nodded. "You should see her. She is one hot mama tonight."

A lustful look entered the guy's eyes and it was all Crow could do not to smack him. But he reminded himself that though Larry could be crude, he'd never let anyone, including himself, take advantage of Sara. That's why Crow had chosen him as his backup.

Crow flipped the guy an extra twenty and waited until he was on his way before heading toward the living room in search of Sara.

"What's going on here?"

Sara turned away from James to the sound of the voice.

Crow stood in the doorway, his dark eyes flashing. Her breath caught in her throat.

Granted, she hadn't known Crow long, but the most dressed up she'd seen him was when he'd worn a polo instead of a T-shirt with his jeans.

Tonight, in a tux that could have been tailor made, he looked positively magnificent. His broad shoulders filled out the jacket to perfection, and with his hair pulled back, she could fully appreciate his chiseled masculine features.

For a brief second a hint of a smile crossed Crow's face at her intense scrutiny. Sara lifted her chin and kept her face expressionless but she had the uneasy feeling he knew just what she'd been thinking.

He raised a sardonic brow. "Didn't your mother teach you it was impolite to stare?"

"Didn't your mother teach you it was impolite to interrupt a private conversation?" she shot back.

Their gazes met and a shiver of excitement shot up Sara's spine. For a moment it was as if no one else existed, no one else mattered.

She was barely aware of James's arm slipping around her shoulder, pulling her firmly to him.

"Sara informs me that you'll be going with us tonight." Though he'd reacted with uncharacteristic anger when she'd told him, James's voice gave no indication that Crow's presence was anything more than an inconvenience.

But Sara knew the proprietary way James held her and his emphasis on "with us" was strictly for Crow's benefit. It shouldn't have surprised her, but it did.

"Do you have a problem with that?" Crow's gaze flickered dismissively over James, telling them all with that simple gesture that he'd do as he'd please, regardless of what either of them wanted.

James's lips tightened and a hint of warning ran through his words. "Not as long as you don't do anything to embarrass Sara."

"Embarrass Sara?" Crow's eyes shone black as coal. "Why would I want to do that?"

* * *

Sara moved through the crowd with James at her elbow. Out of the corner of her eye she could see Crow standing off to the side of the room, leaning against a pillar. He'd been there watching her from a distance most of the evening, a glass of sparkling water in his hand, an inscrutable expression on his face.

She'd hated leaving anyone alone at a party where they knew no one, but he'd assured her he was here as her bodyguard, not as an escort. Her job was to go about her business and forget he was even there.

It was easier said than done. Every time her eyes met his, she reacted like a giddy teen and her heart skipped a beat. Just the thought of his gaze on her made her skin tingle. He liked her dress. The look in his eyes told her that much.

"Sara." James grabbed her arm and his voice was soft and low against her ear. "I see someone you need to meet."

"Who is it?" They'd been mingling for what seemed like hours, and she'd have sworn she'd talked to everyone in the room at least once.

"He's over there. The guy with the attractive brunette." James gestured to a group of people milling around one of the bars. "Do you recognize him?"

It was all Sara could do not to roll her eyes. Recognize who? She counted no less than a dozen men in the area and at least five of them stood next to women who could be considered attractive brunettes, at least from the back.

"Depends on which guy we're talking about," Sara said.

"The one with the blond hair."

Immediately Sara eliminated two guys with dark hair and a bald man in his forties. Two possibilities remained; an athletic-looking guy with sandy-colored hair and an older gentleman whose blond strands were streaked with gray.

As if afraid the man would disappear, James's hand pressed against the small of her back, and he kept his voice low as he hurried her along. "His name is Stephen Comstock and he owns a firm that specializes in business software. I'll introduce you."

"James." Sara planted her feet and refused to budge. "Before I take another step, I want you to tell me what this Stephen Comstock has to do with me."

"You don't recognize the name?" James stared in disbelief. "The guy is a patron of Christian music. I'm hoping we can get him to help sponsor your next tour."

Sara had to smile. This Comstock guy must have

a *lot* of money. It'd been a long time since she'd seen her publicist this excited. "Who's the woman with him? His wife?"

"He's not married." James hesitated. "I think she's his girlfriend. Supposedly he wants to marry her but she's not interested."

"Don't believe everything you hear," Sara said dryly. "Remember when that one tabloid had *us* getting married in Las Vegas on Valentine's Day?"

James grimaced. "Don't remind me."

Sara linked her arm through his and patted his shoulder. The episode had almost put James over the edge. Thankfully the furor over the article and the implication that they were marrying because there was a baby on the way had died a quick death. They never had discovered who'd started the rumor. Or why.

She knew that incident had been partially to blame for his overreaction to the notes. Even though time had shown that the pregnancy and marriage rumors were pure fabrication, James worried that the bad publicity had still affected her career.

"Mr. Comstock." James tapped the younger blond man lightly on the shoulder.

Stephen Comstock looked much too young to be a patron of the arts. Sara guessed he couldn't be more than thirty-two or thirty-three. The gaze he fixed on them was cautious. "Have we met?"

"I'm James Smith with Sara Michaels Enterprises," James said smoothly, shaking his hand. "We met at a golf outing last year."

"Of course." Stephen nodded and recognition filled his gray eyes. He slanted a curious glance at Sara. "Now I know I haven't met you before."

Sara smiled and extended her hand.

Introductions were completed in short order. The man's dark-haired companion had disappeared.

"Stephen, I'm sorry I took so long." The breathless feminine voice sounded behind Sara.

"There you are." Stephen's voice filled with genuine warmth and he reached out to pull the woman to his side.

Sara's eyes widened. "Raven!"

"Sara? I don't believe it." Raven's arms opened and they exchanged a quick hug. "You look fabulous."

Sara graciously accepted the compliment but it was the woman before her who looked fabulous. Raven's hair was pulled back in a low twist and her artfully applied makeup accentuated her high cheekbones. The white dress clung to her like a second skin.

"You two know each other?" James's incredulous gaze shifted from Sara back to Raven.

"Sara and I met through a mutual friend."

She noticed Raven carefully avoided saying Crow's name. Sara wondered if what James had heard was true. Maybe Raven didn't want Stephen because she wanted Crow.

After the introductions were completed, the two men started talking, and Sara decided this was her chance. If she was going to alert Raven, she'd best do it now.

"Crow's here." She kept her tone low enough for Raven's ears only.

"Where?" Raven replied, not even trying to keep her voice down. Her gaze swept the room. "I don't see him."

Either Raven didn't care if Stephen knew about her "friend," or the woman hadn't a clue how to whisper.

"Over there." Sara gestured with her head.

Raven's eyes lit up just as they had this afternoon. She turned to Stephen and squeezed his arm even as her gaze remained fixed on Crow. "I'll be right back. There's someone I need to talk to."

Without waiting for a response, Raven headed across the room.

Sara couldn't keep her gaze from following Raven. Her eyes widened with disbelief when Raven flung her arms around the handsome bodyguard's neck and gave him an effusive hug.

"She knows Crow?" James's shocked voice matched the look on his face.

Sara swallowed hard.

"Who is he?" Stephen asked, taking a sip of his champagne.

"Sara's bodyguard," James said.

"You have a bodyguard?" Stephen's brow furrowed in a frown and he shifted his gaze to Sara.

Stephen seemed more concerned about Crow's vocation than the fact that his arm now rested companionably around Raven's shoulder.

"Just as a preventative measure," James said smoothly. "We thought it wise after the incident involving that singer in Nashville."

"I can understand that," Stephen said.

Sara could almost hear James expel the breath he'd been holding. When he launched into the history of her career, Sara knew they were back on track. Five minutes more and James would be asking for a contribution.

Sara shifted her gaze to the back of the room where Crow and Raven stood talking.

Crow threw back his head and laughed.

Sara's heart clenched.

She liked Raven, she really did. But she didn't like the way the woman was hanging all over Crow. And she really didn't like the fact that Crow didn't seem to mind.

Chapter Seven

"**I** thought we'd stop somewhere and eat." Crow slanted a sideways glance at Sara.

She opened her mouth, ready to say she'd already eaten, but then realized with a start she'd been so busy getting ready for the party, she'd skipped dinner. "I guess I am sort of hungry. What do you have in mind?"

It was after eleven and most of the places she could think of were already closed.

"There's a little café I know across town." He kept his gaze focused on the road but a hint of a smile softened his normally stony expression. "The food is good, but don't expect anything fancy."

An image of a ramshackle diner with cockroaches on the counter and a fly trap over the cash register flashed instantly to mind. "I don't think I'm hungry after all."

Crow's smile widened as if he knew the direction of her thoughts, but surprisingly he didn't try to change her mind. Sara relaxed against the seat and tried to recall if there was enough cold roast beef left in the refrigerator for a sandwich.

Her stomach growled in anticipation and Sara glanced at Crow, half expecting to see a knowing smile. But his eyes were firmly fixed on the road ahead, and if he'd heard the hungry rumblings it didn't show.

They drove in silence until he turned unexpectedly off the main highway.

"This isn't the way to my house." Sara sat upright, more puzzled than alarmed. "Where are you going?"

"I told you. To get us something to eat," he said matter-of-factly.

"I said I'm not hungry." Unfortunately her stomach chose that moment to emit another loud growl.

She lifted her chin and dared him to say anything.

He raised a dark brow and stared.

"Well, maybe I am a little hungry," she said finally. "But I'm not going to eat in any greasy spoon."

"Think you're too good for that kind of place?"

There was no judgment in his dark eyes, just a curious intensity.

"No," she said. "I just prefer my burgers without cockroaches on the side."

To her surprise, he laughed. "Me, too. But seriously if you don't want to eat, don't eat."

"But I—"

"Listen." He cut her off. "We'll eat and leave. Don't tell me you can't spare a half an hour?"

Sara paused and considered his words. They'd already gone so far out of the way, it would be ridiculous to insist they turn back. Still, she was tempted.

"Okay." She leaned back in the plush seat of her Lexus. "But you owe me."

He snorted and she took it as a sign he agreed. Later she'd decide how he could pay her back.

Truth be known, it actually wasn't much of an inconvenience. She'd planned on staying at the party until midnight anyway. But it had wound down early and when James opted to stay, Crow had agreed to take her home.

Though short, the party had been an unqualified success. At least according to James. He'd made several key contacts—the most promising of which was Stephen Comstock.

Sara had been proud watching James in action. All her life she'd dreamed of having such a man at her side—intelligent, handsome, successful and a Christian to boot. If she sometimes felt as if she were playing a role when she was with him, it was a small price to pay. Hopefully one day, if she continued under his tutelage, she'd become the type of woman who would make James as proud of her as she was of him.

James had told her more than once she was perfect just the way she was, but she knew he was concerned about her stubborn steak, her tendency to speak her mind regardless of the costs and her amazing lack of humility. For some reason he couldn't see that those "problem" attributes had been instrumental in helping her get where she was today.

If she wasn't stubbornly determined to rise above the circumstances of her birth, she would have long ago given up her dreams and taken on an eight-to-five job that demanded little and paid even less.

If she didn't believe her voice was a great gift from God and something that shouldn't be wasted, she never would have been able to convince Meg to be her agent and to get those recording executives to give her a chance.

If…

"Here we are." Crow pulled into an unpaved lot and the gravel crunched beneath the tires. "What do you think?"

Sara stared in dismay at the barnlike building. It

was as bad as she'd imagined. With white paint peeling from the weathered siding and windows streaked with grime, it reminded her of the kind of places her mother used to take her. Places filled with smoke and rough-edged men. A shiver traveled up her spine.

"Give it a chance," he said impatiently.

She leaned out the window and took a good look. "I sure hope you're not a person who believes everything you read."

Crow leaned across the seat and followed her gaze to a sign atop the building. Good Food Cheap.

"Well, it's food and it is cheap." His lips twitched. "Two out of three isn't bad. C'mon, let's go inside."

"Remember, I'm not eating." Sara unbuckled her seat belt.

"Suit yourself." He reached for the door latch.

Sara got out of the car without waiting for Crow. Though James always insisted on being a gentleman and opening doors, she couldn't see her bodyguard as the mannerly type. "How in the world did you ever find this place?"

"Angel and I—" he stopped abruptly and began again. "It's a biker place. I've been here a few times."

"Angel? What a pretty name."

He ignored the comment and her questioning look. But her curiosity had been aroused and Sara couldn't wait to continue the conversation once they were seated.

If possible, the interior was worse than she'd imagined. The once black-and-white-checked linoleum floor was now a dingy gray. The fly trap was there; just as she'd imagined, but instead of hanging it over the cash register they'd hung it farther back, close to the kitchen. Though she didn't see any roaches, Sara knew the night was still young.

Crow took a seat and immediately picked up the plastic-coated menu.

Sara brushed the crumbs off the red vinyl seat and wiped the catsup off the edge of the table with a napkin from a chrome dispenser before she slid into the booth.

She leaned forward and rested her elbows on the table. "So, who's Angel?"

Crow slowly raised his gaze. "None of your business."

She offered him an encouraging smile but he'd already returned his attention to the listing of Burgers, Burgers And More Burgers.

Sara narrowed her gaze. Ignoring her never worked, but he'd find that out for himself soon enough. "Just tell me one thing. Is this Angel your girlfriend? Ex-girlfriend? Wife? Ex-wife?"

"I've never been married." He leveled her a

narrowed glinting glance before turning back to the menu. "They've got great pork tenderloins here."

When she just continued to stare, Crow nudged the menu she'd left lying on the table toward her. She shoved it aside without looking down. At the moment, food was the least of her concerns. Besides, one look at the place had convinced her it would be a cold day in hell before she ate here.

"How come you're not married?" she said in her most persuasive manner. "You're certainly old enough. How old are you anyway? Thirty-nine? Forty?"

He couldn't be more than thirty but she wanted a reaction. Any reaction.

Crow laid his menu on the table and heaved an irritated sigh. "I'm thirty-two."

Sara smiled to herself. Interrogating him was turning out to be a piece of cake. Flushed with success she pressed on. "All I want to know is if Angel is your current girlfriend or not? What's so hard about that?"

Crow lifted his gaze. For a second she swore she saw a hint of amusement in the dark depths. "You don't give up easily, do you?"

"It's part of my charm." She tossed her head. "C'mon, fess up. Current or ex?"

"Angel's an old friend. Nothing more."

"Do I look stupid?"

"I'm serious." He shook his head. "In some ways you remind me of her."

"Oh, yeah?" She leaned forward, eager to hear more.

"Yeah," Crow said, lifting his gaze. "She never knew when to shut up, either."

Sara decided she liked the woman already.

"And she's stubborn as a mule."

The woman rose another notch in Sara's estimation. "Think you two might get together one day?"

"No way," he said.

"Why not? Couples split up and get back together all the time."

"I already told you we were never a couple." He raised a hand and gestured for the waitress. "You'd better take a look at the menu."

Time was running out. She switched gears. "When did you start dating Raven? Before or after Angel?"

"Are you crazy?" The expression on Crow's face would have been laughable if he hadn't bellowed so loud, the guys at the bar turned to look.

"Keep your voice down," Sara whispered fiercely. The last thing she needed was to cause a scene. "Why deny it? I've seen you two together. It's obvious she means a lot to you."

Crow unclipped his tie and loosened the collar of his shirt. "What's it to you, anyway?"

Sara shrugged. "I just want to know, that's all."

"You guys ready to order?" The waitress had jet-black hair, a butterfly tattooed on her right forearm and a tiny ring in her nose.

Sara considered pointing out to Crow that he and the woman had a lot in common, but she decided not to push her luck. "I'll have an iced tea."

"Two pork tenderloins, a large order of fries and a pitcher of beer," Crow said.

Sara lifted an eyebrow. How he could keep such a lean and muscular body when eating like that was beyond her.

It wasn't until the woman brought the beer with two glasses and Crow filled both and slid one across the table to her that she realized he'd meant for them to share the pitcher.

She stared at the glass, sorely tempted. "This is for me?"

"Of course it's for you." He took a long sip and studied her quizzically. "Who else?"

Sara lifted her damp hair off the back of her neck. If the café had air-conditioning, she couldn't feel it. She gazed longingly at the mug. Foam topped the amber liquid and condensation dotted the outside of the glass.

Sara swallowed hard. She'd always liked the taste of beer. However, since James had come on board as her publicist, Sara hadn't had so much as a sip.

Although many Christians had no problem with drinking as long as it was in moderation, some did. And James's argument was why should she risk offending some of her supporters?

She battled with him over it, not because alcohol was so important to her, but if she wanted a glass of wine with dinner or an occasional beer, she didn't see why she should deprive herself. In the end she'd given in, not so much because she agreed he was right but because she'd decided to pick her battles. And this one hadn't been that important.

Her gaze slid around the café. Other than a couple of biker types and the waitress, who was sitting on a bar stool smoking a cigarette, she and Crow had the place to themselves. Not a fan or reporter in sight.

Sara lifted the glass and took a sip, licking the foam from her lips. "How'd you know I liked beer?"

He shrugged. "Doesn't everyone?"

"James doesn't think I should drink."

"My great-grandfather used to think a man wasn't a man unless he chewed." Crow shrugged and took another sip of his beer.

"Chewing tobacco?" Sara grimaced. "I'm glad you didn't take your grandfather's message to heart."

He grinned and gestured to her now-half-empty

mug. "And I'm glad you didn't take James's words to heart."

The waitress chose that moment to appear with the sandwiches, and this time Sara didn't even blink when the woman set one before her. Her mouth was too busy watering at the sight of the breaded pork sticking out from the sides of the sesame bun.

Crow handed her the mustard and she squirted it in a figure eight across the top of the meat.

In a matter of seconds, she found herself munching happily on her sandwich and talking to Crow as if she'd known him all her life.

It wasn't that he was a great conversationalist. In fact, quite the opposite was true. He listened far more than he talked, asking just enough questions to keep her rattling on about herself.

Sara barely noticed when he poured her another beer, leaving his own glass empty. And when the fries and tenderloins were gone and the dishes cleared away, the two remained at the table.

She'd never laughed so much. Or talked so much. She found Crow incredibly easy to talk to and quite charming. He didn't even seem to mind when she rambled. Although she hadn't revealed anything significant, it'd been a long time since Sara had opened up so much to a stranger.

It wasn't until they were back in the car that it

occurred to her that she'd been the one doing most of the drinking. And the talking.

And Crow had done most of the asking. And the listening.

Her heart sank to her feet.

He'd spent the evening pumping her for information and she'd been stupid enough to give it to him.

Chapter Eight

"**I** knew it was a long shot, Harvey." Crow spoke directly into the receiver and kept his voice low. Though he was alone in the den, this wasn't a conversation he wanted Sara to overhear.

Harvey, the director of the police department's forensic unit, chuckled. "You were right. Those notes had more fingerprints on 'em than a door handle at Wal-Mart."

Crow couldn't help but smile at the comparison. Harvey loved Wal-Mart. He always said if they didn't have what you were looking for, it wasn't worth having. "Thanks for checking anyway."

"No problem," Harvey said. "Just try 'n' get me a better sample next time."

"I'll do my best." Crow hung up and leaned

back in the chair, barely noticing the softness of the overstuffed cushions. Sara's den had been furnished with comfort in mind, but the room's quiet solitude brought him little comfort or peace.

When would he quit hoping for miracles? Granted, a good fingerprint on the note was a long shot. But even long shots sometimes paid off.

He'd risen early to call Harvey, hoping for good news. Instead he'd hit another dead end.

Crow took a sip of his now-lukewarm coffee. The investigation was going nowhere. First, he only had the unsigned notes to work off of; the envelopes had been pitched so he didn't have a postmark. Then everybody and his dog had handled them, shooting down any chance of isolating a good print. Finally, to top it all off, Sara refused to talk about it, insisting it was just a prank.

Crow found her reluctance to discuss the issue strange, to say the least. Any woman would be concerned about receiving such notes. And while Sara could talk about inconsequential things at length, she refused to speculate about who might be behind the threats. Unfortunately he had to go easy with his interrogations. To her he was only a bodyguard, not a cop.

Last weekend when they'd stopped at the diner, Crow had hoped a few beers would loosen her up and make his job easier. But instead of talking about the note, she'd talked about everything else.

When he'd gotten home that night, he would have said he knew all there was to know about Sara Michaels. But the next morning on further reflection, he'd realized she'd told him little more than she'd already told a half-dozen reporters.

Though he knew she'd gone into foster care at fifteen, he still didn't understand why. Sara was a master at making a vague answer seem plausible. But he was a professional and he shouldn't have been satisfied with less than the whole story. If he hadn't been mesmerized by the fullness of her lips and the way her husky voice made his gut clench, he might have seized the moment and gotten some real information out of her. Instead he'd wasted the whole evening wondering what it would be like to kiss her again.

And even now, when his thoughts should be focused on business, he couldn't help but reflect on the sweetness of her lips and wonder if today was the day he'd get that second kiss.

Sara stared at the calendar on her dresser and slowly pulled the brush through her hair. She had several hours before she had to be at the studio, and she'd decided to relax. Without a thousand and one things on her mind, her thoughts kept returning to those blasted notes.

She knew Meg was desperately worried. If Sara didn't know who was behind the notes, she might have agreed with Meg's suggestion that the police should be involved. But having someone snooping around was the last thing she needed. So she'd tried to placate Meg by telling her that she was sure it was only a joke and they would be foolish to overreact.

Deep down, Sara knew another would be coming. The only question was *when*. Every day she waited anxiously for the mail and every day she breathed a sigh of relief when there was no note in the pile of bills and solicitations. Could it be that Gary had grown tired of his little game and decided to leave her alone? Her heart quickened at the thought and she had to fight to still the rising hope. She couldn't be so lucky.

Letting her off easy wasn't Gary's style. After all, he was a man who'd once boasted that he'd slashed the tires of an ex-girlfriend's car when she'd refused his phone call. She could only hope that he'd moved out of state. Or was back in prison.

Sara swallowed hard. She was kidding herself. Gary hadn't gone away. He was still out there somewhere, watching and waiting, laughing that he was making her sweat.

How long had it been since she'd seen him? More than a decade probably. She'd been fourteen and a freshman in high school. Gary had been her mother's live-in boyfriend. He was a big man, six feet four inches, with dark shaggy hair and a beard and mustache that always needed trimming. He worked construction and had the stamina of an ox.

Though Gary had never touched her, his eyes always glowed with a malevolent gleam, and Sara made it a point never to be alone with him. Her mother thought the guy walked on water, and in their house, his word was law.

Like in the matter of the dress. Sara's first high school dance had been fast approaching and she didn't have anything to wear that was even remotely suitable. Gary and her mother always had enough for alcohol and cigarettes so Sara figured they could spare a few dollars for a dress.

She'd waited patiently for the perfect opportunity to ask her mother. Finally she couldn't wait any longer. The dance was two days away.

That night would always be clear in her mind. Even after all these years she remembered the hot stickiness in their third-floor walk-up apartment.

It was a Thursday night in late September...

* * *

Sara glanced at the clock. It was past ten and she was determined to ask her mother tonight. But it would have to be soon, before her mother and Gary left for the bar. When they got home, neither of them would be in any shape to answer a question. Plus all indications were it would be a late night. Gary had won big at the casino and he was in the mood to party.

"Mom?" Sara paused at her mother's bedroom door and rapped lightly. She'd made the mistake of barging in once without knocking and her cheeks still burned with the memory of what she'd seen. "Can I come in? There's something I need to talk to you about."

"Sure, honey." Her mother sounded surprisingly happy and Sara's hopes rose.

She opened the door and slipped into the room. Her mother sat at the vanity table she'd made out of an old desk, reapplying her makeup. Gary was sprawled out on the bed, still wearing the ragged jeans and T-shirt that he'd worn to work that day. Sara resisted the urge to point out that if anyone needed a makeover, it was Gary.

"Uh, this is personal." Sara glanced at him, hoping he'd catch the drift and leave.

"Gary and I don't have any secrets," her mother said, swiping her lashes with another coat of mascara.

"That's right, and don't you forget it, either." Gary propped himself on one elbow, letting his gaze linger.

Suddenly Sara's shorts seemed too short and the modest V of her cotton T-shirt too low. She resisted the urge to tug on her shorts and place one hand over the lowest part of the V.

The jerk smirked as if he knew the direction of her thoughts. She lifted her chin and turned away.

"Mom, I have a favor to ask." Sara kept her voice low and spoke quickly. "Could I—"

"If it involves money, the answer is no," Gary said loudly from the bed, punching the remote and blasting the room with hard rock music.

"Could you turn that down?" Sara's hands clenched into fists and she glared at Gary. "We're trying to talk here."

"Sara!" Her mother's gaze darkened. "Show some respect. This is Gary's house, too."

Since when? Sara wanted to ask, but she bit her tongue. She couldn't afford to blow this opportunity. The dance was Saturday night.

"I'm sorry." Sara shot Gary an insincere smile before turning her attention to her mother. "I don't know if you remember me talking about this dance at school? The Freshman Frolic?"

Her mother's makeup brush stilled for a moment before she shook her head. "No. I don't think you said anything to me. Maybe you mentioned it to Gary.''

Yeah, right. As if I'd ever talk to him about anything important.

''Anyway—'' Sara forced a cheery smile ''—it's Saturday night, and it's the biggest dance of the year for freshmen. Everyone is wearing those dresses, you know the ones with—''

''Stop right there,'' Gary interrupted, waving a beer in one hand. ''I told you if you're asking for money, the answer is no.''

''I'm not talking to you,'' Sara snapped.

Gary's gaze turned steely and an uneasy silence descended. Sara's mother's fingers whitened around the handle of her brush. ''Sara, you shouldn't speak to Gary that way. Tell him you're sorry.''

''I'm not sorry.'' Sara glared at him. ''This is none of his business.''

''This is my house,'' Gary said in an ominous tone. His brows pulled together like two dark thunderclouds. ''And you better not forget it.''

''You are *so* stupid,'' Sara said, deciding to tell it like it was, knowing the money was as good as gone anyway. ''This isn't a house, it's an apartment. And, for your information it's *our* apartment, not yours.''

''You wait a minute here. I pay—''

"Don't even go there." Sara ground out the words between clenched teeth. All the anger and frustration she'd buried this past year rose like a volcano from deep inside. "You haven't paid on the rent since forever. If it was up to me, you'd be out on your butt faster than you can say 'get me another beer.'"

"Why you little—" Gary plunked the beer on the table with a thud and swung his legs over the side of the bed.

"Gary, honey, she didn't mean no harm. Did you, Sara?" Fear filled her mother's eyes and her look begged Sara to agree.

Seeing Gary's murderous glance and his hands clenched into fists, Sara had no choice but to back down. Though she'd never felt the repercussions of Gary's temper, her mother had, and Sara would do anything to prevent that from happening again.

"I didn't mean any harm." Sara nearly choked on the words. She forced an apologetic smile. "Honest."

"Yeah, right." Gary's gaze shifted from Sara to her mother. "What about you, Ilene? Do you agree with your daughter? Do you think I'm a worthless bum?"

"Of course not, Gary," her mother answered so promptly, Sara wondered if she'd even heard the question or had just decided to agree with whatever he said.

"I work hard for my money," Gary said, his gaze daring her to disagree. "And I can spend it any way I like."

"Of course you can, sweetheart." Her mother lined her upper and lower lids with extra kohl just the way Gary liked. "We all know how hard you work."

Sara remained silent.

"I work a lot harder than that Mike Richards does in that fancy office of his," Gary said, his expression calculating.

"Mike Richards?" Sara asked, wishing immediately after seeing her mother's face that she could take the question back. Even though she'd never heard his name, Sara realized too late that this must be the guy her mother met when Gary worked overtime.

"Just someone that works down at the plant," her mother said. "We're friends, that's all."

"Well, you tell your *friend* you got a man and he better keep his hands to himself."

For the first time Sara noticed that Gary's words were slurred. The beer he'd been drinking was obviously not his first this evening.

"You're my woman, not his. And you and your

friend Mike better not forget it." Gary punched the pillow hard.

Her mother smiled easily but Sara was close enough to see the trembling in her hands. "I don't need to tell him that, Gary. I've already made it clear."

"Good." Seemingly satisfied, Gary belched and settled back against the pillows, reaching for the beer he'd set aside.

Though Sara estimated her chances now to be close to a million to one, she decided to give it one last shot. She lowered her voice almost to a whisper and bent close to her mother's ear. "Could you please lend me forty dollars for the dress? I promise I'll pay you back. Mrs. Kent down the hall wants me to baby-sit. I'll give you—"

"I thought I made myself clear." Gary flipped off the stereo and his voice cut the sudden silence like a knife. "No money."

Sara tried to ignore him but she couldn't, any more than she could ignore the tightness gripping her chest in a stranglehold. She wanted that dress more than she'd ever wanted anything.

"Mom?" She shot her mother an imploring gaze.

Sara saw the answer in her mother's eyes long before she spoke.

"I'm sorry, Sara," her mother said. "But Gary's the head of this household and what he says goes."

"But that's not fair," Sara wailed. She cooked, she cleaned and she got nothing in return.

"That's the way it is," her mother said. "Maybe—"

"No maybe. The answer is no. Quit coddling her, Ilene." Gary stared at Sara, his red-rimmed eyes glittering. "I don't 'preciate your back talk. My daddy gave me a good whoppin' when I talked back to him."

Gary reached for his belt buckle and unfastened it, his glassy eyes riveted to Sara.

Sara stood frozen, horrified.

"Sara, go to your room. Now." Her mother's no-nonsense voice broached no argument, and though an uneasy strain edged her eyes, the smile she shot Gary was warm and inviting. "Gary and I have things to do, places to go. Don't we, sweetheart?"

Sara fled the room, tears pushing against the back of her lids. She'd rather die than let them see her cry. She hated it when Gary laughed at her, and when her mother joined him.

But it was too late. The sounds of their laughter followed her down the hall and into her room.

They'd be sorry, she vowed. She deserved that dress and she was going to have it. She'd seen

Gary's wallet lying on the dresser, bulging with money. In a few days the booze and lottery tickets would have it all unless she acted quickly. She just had to make sure she didn't get caught....

"Sara, the mail is here."

The knock at the door jerked Sara from her reverie.

She jumped up from the dressing table, banging her knee on the edge. Hobbling quickly to the door she flung it open.

Annie, a graduate student who worked as a part-time housekeeper in exchange for a small salary and room and board, stood in the hall. Her sunny smile faded when she saw Sara. "Are you okay?"

"I'm fine." Despite the stabbing pain in her leg, Sara forced a smile. "Just bumped my knee."

Annie held out a thick wad of envelopes. "You said you wanted to see the mail as soon as it arrived."

"Thanks for bringing it up to me, Annie. I really appreciate it." Sara took the mail and resisted the urge to flip through it right then. "By the way, have you seen Crow this morning?"

"He was on the phone when I last saw him." Annie paused for a second. "You know that bodyguard of yours is one good-looking man."

"You think so?" Sara stared in surprise. She'd

never thought of Crow as Annie's type. "What about all that hair?"

"Not a problem." An impish twinkle shone in Annie's eyes and Sara realized with a jolt that though she'd always thought of Annie as older, the woman couldn't be more than thirty. That would make her only five years older than Sara and right around Crow's age. "A few snips of the scissors and it'd be history."

Sara chuckled, imagining Crow's reaction. "What about the tattoo?"

"The barbed wire thing?"

Sara nodded. Annie was straight as an arrow. The woman didn't even pierce her ears. She had to be horrified by that tattoo encircling Crow's bicep.

Annie lifted one shoulder in a careless shrug. "I like it."

"You do not." Sara widened her eyes in disbelief.

"I do." Annie's face flushed bright red. "I think it's kind of sexy."

Sara laughed as if the idea was ridiculous even though if pressed she'd have to admit the tattoo didn't repel her as much as it once did. But sexy? "You do not think a tattoo is sexy."

Annie nodded, a tiny smile tugging at the corners of her lips, a sheepish expression on her face.

"I find Crow incredibly appealing. All that wild dark hair, those gorgeous eyes…"

"I know, I know." Sara waved her silent. "I have to admit he is kind of hot."

"Who's hot?"

Sara whirled at the familiar voice and the laughter died in her throat. How much had Crow heard? And what was she going to say if he'd heard too much?

Chapter Nine

Sara decided Annie should have been in politics. Without missing a beat, her housekeeper smiled warmly and batted her long lashes. "We were discussing the stove. I think the pilot light has gone out."

She batted her eyes again and this time Sara knew it was no accident. Annie was flirting with Crow!

Irritated, Sara scowled at her housekeeper, but Annie was too focused on Crow to notice.

Annie would soon realize that Crow wasn't the kind of man who liked women fawning all over him. And he certainly would never be attracted to a woman who played at being a helpless female.

Oddly the thought pleased Sara, and she was just about to suggest they all grab a bite of breakfast when she heard Annie mention how much she liked his tattoo.

Crow glanced at Sara with a smug smile.

Sara snorted in disgust.

"Did you say something, Sara?" Crow lifted a brow and she swore she saw laughter in his gaze.

"No." Sara made a great production of clearing her throat, determined not to give him any satisfaction. "I was just going to say, why don't you help Annie with that pilot light? I've got to finish getting ready and then you can take me to the studio."

His gaze lingered on her face, then dropped to her chenille robe.

Sara kept her gaze steady and even managed to offer Annie a smile.

After all, her housekeeper *had* done her a favor and it wouldn't do to forget it. Annie had intercepted the mail and brought it to Sara without Crow or Meg being the wiser. And her flirting had given Sara the time she needed to stick the mail deep inside the oversize pocket of her robe.

"I better get the coffee cake out of the oven." Annie headed toward the stairs, casting a backward glance at Crow.

"I'll be right down." Crow kept his gaze fixed on Sara.

"I'll be waiting," Annie called out cheerfully.

"When will you be ready?" Crow didn't even

acknowledge that Annie had left and he seemed in no hurry to follow her downstairs. "Fifteen minutes?"

"Give me thirty," Sara said, backing slowly toward her door. "I'm not through with my makeup yet and I still have to dress."

His eyes met hers and a strange tension filled the air. "You look fine to me."

Sara moistened her suddenly dry lips. "Do I?"

"I think you do."

Sara stared.

He took a step forward.

She kept her eyes focused on him and swallowed hard.

He took another step forward.

Her heart pounded against her ribs and she couldn't have moved if she'd wanted to.

His final step closed the last of the distance between them. Now he was so close, she could have reached out and touched him, if she dared.

The spicy smell of his cologne wafted over her and she inhaled, deeply reveling in the masculine scent. From where she stood she could feel his warmth and almost taste the sweetness of his lips.

Sara took a step forward and lifted her face. Would this one be as good as the first?

Her pulse skittered and she held her breath.

He lowered his head.

"Are you coming or not?" Annie's irritated

voice from the bottom of the stairs had the effect of a splash of cold water.

Crow immediately stepped back, his face expressionless.

A wave of heat rose up Sara's neck.

"I'd better go help her." Crow turned toward the stairs. No one watching him would believe only moments before he'd been as caught up in the moment as she had. But she remembered his eyes burning like hot coals and she knew he'd wanted that kiss as much as she did.

Had she *ever* felt that way about kissing James? Sara didn't have to think twice to answer that question. No one stirred her senses like Crow. She shoved aside a twinge of guilt and returned to her room, focusing instead on the mail burning a hole in her pocket.

Sara plopped down on her bed and pulled out the envelopes, dropping them onto the quilt. Junk mail, bills and personal correspondence scattered everywhere.

Then she saw it. It was a tiny envelope, the size of a wedding invitation. The envelope had no return address and Sara knew there would be no invitation inside.

For a moment she felt lightheaded. She took several deep breaths before glancing at the postmark. It had been mailed in St. Louis, just like the others. Her fingers trembled, and she could barely break the seal. Inside would be a threat; that was a given. But would it be more specific than the others? And would Gary actually have the guts to sign this one?

Sara took another deep breath and pulled the note from the envelope. In a second she had it unfolded.

She stared unblinking at the words: Judgment Day is near. You will pay for your sins.

Sara flung the sheet of paper on the bed. The nerve of the guy. If anyone deserved to pay for his sins it was Gary Burke.

Leaving the note for the moment on the bed, Sara rose and quickly finished dressing. Every time her eyes strayed to the note, she forced herself to think of her upcoming recording session, on James's plans for her career, on the way Crow filled out his jeans, anything but on the note and Gary Burke. Nothing would be accomplished by worrying.

This note was no worse than the others. But it did confirm one fact she should never have doubted.

Gary was back in her life.

And he wouldn't leave her alone until he had gotten his revenge.

"So, did you get that pilot light lit?"

Crow heard Sara's footsteps before her voice. He lazily lifted his gaze, his lips widening into an appreciative smile. The cornflower blue of the dress she'd chosen accentuated the blue of her eyes while the clingy fabric highlighted her curves. She looked, he thought idly, like every man's idea of heavenly. "Did you have any doubts?"

Sara smiled and shook her head. "Where's Annie?"

"She said something about being late to class." He shrugged. "I thought I'd have a cup of coffee before we left. Care to join me?"

"Since this is my house—" her smile came easy and took any sting from the words "—shouldn't I be the one asking you?"

He chuckled. "I don't think either of us minds breaking a few rules."

For an instant Sara flushed as if he'd hit a nerve, but then one hand rose to her heart and when she spoke her voice was melodramatic and slightly teasing. "Speak for yourself, mister. I'm as straight as they come."

Even if the twinkle in her eye hadn't given her away, he'd come to know her too well the last couple of weeks to fall for a line like that.

"What about the beer?" he asked innocently.

"What beer?"

"How soon they forget." Crow's grin widened. "The pitcher we shared at the diner last weekend?"

"Oh, that." Sara waved a dismissive hand. "I had one glass. So what?"

He raised a brow. "One?"

"Okay, maybe two." A slight flush crept up her neck, but her shrug was nonchalant. "You had a few, too."

She'd had more like three, while he'd kept to only one, knowing he'd be driving home. But she'd been so busy talking, he doubted she'd noticed. "Unlike you, I don't need to justify my actions."

"And you think I do?"

"Not to me," he said smoothly, surprised to hear the edge in her voice. "But to others, maybe. After all, you're Sara Michaels. People watch what you do. I'm just along for the ride. I can bend the rules. Break them even. Nobody cares, much less notices."

"I disagree,". Sara said softly. "God notices. He cares."

Crow stirred uncomfortably, thinking of some of his actions the last few years that he'd just as soon God *didn't* notice while at the same time wondering how Sara had managed to once again shift the focus back on him. "I'm sure God has more important things to do than to watch me."

"So you *do* believe?" Sara slipped into the seat opposite him and leaned forward. "You're not an atheist."

"Of course I'm not an atheist." His faith may have been seriously shaken, but he could no more be an atheist than he could be a vegetarian.

"Great." The worry that had clouded her gaze faded and her blue eyes sparkled with an irrepressible missionary zeal. "You can go with me to church on Sunday."

Crow groaned to himself and forced a noncommittal smile. He'd taken the last few Sundays off and had one of the backup bodyguards pull the church duty. He might have to do that again.

"Sunday's a long way off." He rose and reached out his hand. "Let's get some breakfast. I'm starving."

She made no move to take his hand. "If you prefer, we could go to your church?"

"I don't have one."

"Then it's settled," she said with satisfaction. "We'll go to mine."

An expletive slipped past his lips.

Her eyes widened. "Am I to take that to mean you don't want to go?"

"You got it," he said.

"You say you're a believer, yet you don't want to go to church. I guess I don't understand where you're coming from," she said, half to herself. Her gaze lingered on his hair before dropping to his tattoo.

She paused. "Tell me something, Crow. Do you

believe that as a Christian you should follow God's law?''

''I know I should be going to church, if that's what you mean.''

She laughed, a husky throaty laugh. ''That's part of it. But there's more to it than that. Come on, just humor me.''

He plopped down in the chair. It looked like breakfast was going to have to wait. ''You mean like the ten commandments?''

''Yes, like the commandments.''

Crow thought quickly, not sure he wanted to get into a religious discussion. But he decided the question was more philosophical in nature. ''If you're asking if I see things as black and white, in absolutes, the answer is no.''

Sara raised a brow. ''Are you saying that sometimes it's okay to kill? Or to…or lust after your neighbor's wife?''

Her expression remained impassive, but her gaze was sharp with interest.

Crow hadn't set foot in a church in several years. It had been even longer since he'd thought about the commandments. His answer obviously hadn't been what she'd expected. But he'd never been one to tell a woman something just because she wanted to hear it.

''If you're asking if I would ever make a play for a married woman, the answer is no.'' Lusting after someone's wife had never occurred to him. As a little boy, he didn't understand what "covet" meant, and as an adult he respected marriage vows too much to ever let his thoughts go in that direction.

"But in terms of killing, I'm a bodyguard. Why would I carry a gun if I wouldn't use it?" He paused. "Don't get me wrong. I think the commandments are a good way to live. And other than killing, I think most can be regarded as absolutes."

"Even stealing?"

He could tell she regretted asking the question the minute the words left her lips. He didn't blame her. He didn't want to prolong the discussion, either. A little bit went a long way on an empty stomach. Thankfully she'd given him an easy question this time. A plate of ham and eggs were as good as his.

"Stealing?" He met her gaze head-on. "That's easy. If a person's survival were at stake, I might be able to excuse it. But other than that I can't see where stealing would ever be justified."

I can't see where stealing would ever be justified.

Sara told herself if Crow knew why she'd originally started stealing money from her mother's boyfriends, he would understand. After all, her fear of being homeless had been a powerful motivation.

But it was that last forty dollars that even Sara found hard to justify. Because what she'd done went beyond stealing. It was pure selfishness. Pure vanity and greed had led her to steal. And because of it, she'd nearly killed her own mother.

The events of the morning haunted her thoughts and she found it difficult to concentrate at breakfast. But thankfully once she reached the studio and shut the door to the isolation booth, she was able to block everything out but the music.

Though Crow had wanted to be with her in the studio, she was glad she'd insisted he wait in the lobby. It was hard to concentrate when he was around. This album was too important, and the last thing she needed was to be distracted. After six hours of hard work, her producer told her he was convinced they had a good one.

Exhausted, Sara could only smile with relief. She loved to sing but the recording part sometimes got a bit intense. Her new CD was scheduled for a fall release and winning the Sheldon Award had only increased the pressure.

After thanking the musicians and backup singers, Sara grabbed her purse and headed over to where James stood. He rarely came to the studio when she was recording but she'd seen him slip into the production booth toward the end of the session.

"That sounded great," James said, brushing a kiss across her cheek.

"You think it'll be good?"

"It'll be fabulous." His voice was filled with confidence. "I don't know why you're so worried. This is your third album, not your first."

"Yes, but my fans expect more now." The sick feeling in the pit of Sara's stomach that had been there earlier returned. "A bad album could ruin it all."

"It's not going to be bad," James said. "And even so, worst-case scenario, one bad album won't destroy your career."

"Yeah, right."

"I'm serious," he said, meeting her gaze. His expression softened at the worry she knew must be in her eyes. "Just remember, more careers are destroyed by bad press than by one bad album."

Bad press.

"That's supposed to make me feel better?"

"It should," James said. "You've got a great reputation, both personally and professionally. I know you've heard me say it a thousand times but I'll say it again. Image is everything. You can bounce back from a few mediocre songs, but ruin that reputation and you could be out for good."

"What happened to good old-fashioned Christian forgiveness?" Sara forced a lighthearted laugh.

"People are funny." James paused for a moment. "They'll forgive friends and family, but if their heroes disappoint them, they can be vicious."

"Vicious, eh?" Sara widened her eyes in mock surprise. "I hope they never turn on me."

"Why would they?" A warm fondness reflected in James's gaze. "You're as good as they come. Practically perfect."

If he only knew.

"What if I wasn't?" Sara lifted her gaze. Was it finally time to come clean? Her heart pounded in her chest and she resisted the urge to wipe her damp palms against her dress. "Perfect, I mean?"

She'd never planned to lie to James. Ever since he'd taken over as her publicist, she'd wanted to be straight with him. But what would he say if he knew the truth?

James stared at her for a long moment. Suddenly he laughed. "You're good. For a second you really had me going."

She swallowed hard. "I did?"

"For one wild instant I actually thought you had some deep dark secret that you hadn't told me." His arm stole around her shoulder. "Don't scare me like that."

This was her cue to laugh and toss off some remark that the only deep dark secret she had was that she used to have a crush on Jordan of New

Kids on the Block fame. But she couldn't bring
herself to speak, much less laugh.

"Sara?" A frown furrowed James's brow. "You
were just joking, weren't you?"

Dear God, what choice do I have but to lie?

You always have choices, a tiny voice deep inside whispered. Sara silenced it immediately.
James didn't want the truth. That was obvious.
Some things were best left unsaid. Some secrets
were best left buried.

Her hand slipped into her pocket and she fingered the note. Why couldn't Gary have stayed in
the past where he belonged? And why didn't he
get to the point, saying what he wanted instead of
making veiled threats? Even as she asked the question, Sara knew the answer. Gary didn't want to
just make her pay; he wanted her to bleed.

A cold chill ran down her spine but she forced
a reassuring smile.

"Oh, James, don't be silly. Of course I was joking." The calmness of her voice amazed even
Sara. "I have nothing to hide. Nothing at all."

Chapter Ten

Crow stared across the dining room table. Sara was hiding something, he decided. All day long she'd been nervous as a cat.

If they'd been alone, he would have tried to draw her out, ask a few questions and discover what was bothering her. But Meg and James had both stayed for dinner and James had monopolized the conversation, raving about some fabulous promotional campaign that he'd planned to coincide with the release of the new CD.

Not even Crow could fault James's work ethic. The guy gave one hundred ten percent to his job. The thing that bothered Crow was when James talked about Sara's career, it was as if the career were his client, not Sara herself.

"Would anyone care for dessert?" Sara glanced

around the table. "I think there's some cherry pie."

"Dinner was wonderful." Meg dropped her napkin to her plate. "But I'm afraid I'll have to pass. I've still got some phone calls to return and it's getting late."

"None for me, either." James shook his head. "Just talking about this promotion spurred some new ideas. I'm going back to the office for a few hours."

"I'm fine, too," Crow said. "But if you want some…?"

"I'm way too full," Sara said quickly.

Crow's gaze shifted to her plate. Though chicken cordon bleu was one of her favorites, she hadn't eaten more than a few bites of it and had only picked at the rest of her food. Something was definitely up. Crow slanted a look at James. Could there be trouble in paradise?

The thought lifted his spirits momentarily before reality intervened. Although Sara had been quieter than normal during the meal, there had been no signs of tension between her and James.

It had been business as usual. Meg and Crow had eaten silently while Sara's attention had remained focused on James.

Crow hadn't heard a word. He'd tuned James out and had focused all his attention on Sara. On how pretty she looked with her blond hair falling in soft curls past her shoulders and a dab of glossy pink color on her mouth. His lips still burned with the memory of the kiss they'd shared.

"I'm going to walk James to the door," Sara announced. She pushed back her chair and stood.

Meg and Crow exchanged glances. Only when the two were out of earshot, did Meg speak. "What she sees in that man is beyond me."

"He seems to have a good head on his shoulders," Crow said finally.

"He's done some positive things for her image, I'll grant you that," Meg said. "But I'm talking on a more personal level."

"That's not my business." Crow mouthed the appropriate, though insincere, reply. "My business is protecting her and finding out who's behind the note."

"Speaking of the note, how did the fingerprint thing go?" Meg said softly.

"No luck." Crow dropped his own voice a notch. "I just—"

"What are you two whispering about?" Sara stood in the archway, hands on her hips with her blue eyes flashing.

The look in Meg's eyes told Crow Sara's sudden reappearance had caught the woman by surprise. For Crow, one of the advantages to working undercover was that very few things escaped his notice. Or caught him off guard.

"Whispering?" Crow raised a brow. "I don't whisper."

"Sara, we were just talking." Meg's voice resonated with the right amount of indignation.

"Sorry." Sara raked a hand through her hair. Even though it was barely past eight, tiny lines of fatigue edged her eyes. "Your voices just sounded really low, and when I—" She stopped herself. "Forget it. I was wrong. I apologize."

Meg peered at Sara intently, a look of concern on her face. "You seem stressed. Bad day?"

So Meg had noticed it, too.

Sara shook her head. "Not really. The recording session went great. Actually it couldn't have gone better. I think I'm just a little tired."

"I know what you need." Meg's smile was more motherly than that of a manager. "A nice long soak in the tub. You could use some of those expensive bath oils we picked up in New York."

"I may do that later." Sara rubbed her neck with the back of her hand. "Right now I think I'll go down to the gazebo for a while."

"I'm ready." Crow pushed back his chair and rose.

"Actually, I prefer to go alone," Sara said. "I have a song in my head that I need to get down on paper."

"I didn't realize you wrote your own music," Crow said.

"There's more to Sara than meets the eye." Meg's smile was filled with pride.

Sara glanced at the door. "I'm sorry to cut this short. But I've got to get this song down. I'm sure you understand."

Crow studied her for a moment. He understood all right. He understood completely. She was hiding something.

"I won't bother you," he said. "You won't even know I'm there."

"No." Sara spoke so sharply, even Meg raised a brow. "I mean, that won't work."

"I won't say a word." Crow held up both hands palm out. "Promise."

She shook her head firmly. "Just having you there will be a distraction."

"It's not safe." Though he wanted to be with her, her safety was his primary concern. Although well lit, the gazebo stood a good thirty feet from the house, surrounded by tall bushes and trees. "You shouldn't be out there by yourself."

His tone broached no argument.

"Crow," Meg said soothingly, her gaze shifting between him and Sara, "She'll be okay. The backyard has a security fence and the gazebo is just a stone's throw from the house."

"I don't like it." Crow crossed his arms across his chest. "Too many—"

"The subject is closed." Sara's blue eyes

flashed. "You work for me, remember? I *will* go to the gazebo and I *will* go alone. If something happens to me, I take full responsibility."

There were a thousand arguments he could have given her but he didn't waste his breath. He could see the effort would be futile. On the outside Sara might look like an angel, but inside she was pure mule, stubborn and hardheaded.

"You really think you can take care of yourself?" he scoffed.

"I have for years." She met his challenging gaze with one of her own. "Why should now be any different?"

The gazebo had always been Sara's refuge, the place she came to when she needed solace, a place to gather her thoughts and reflect.

Tonight Sara had a lot to think about. She hadn't lied to Crow. There *was* a verse that she wanted to get down on paper. But this evening her reason for coming to the gazebo had nothing to do with a new song and everything to do with the note in her pocket.

Sara pulled it out and stared down at the folded sheet. Gary was getting close to making his move. And she needed to be prepared.

How would he do it? she wondered. Wait until he caught her alone? Or confront her when she was in a crowd?

If Gary went the public route, odds were he'd be overpowered immediately. He was smart enough to know that. No, he'd definitely try to find her alone.

Like I am now.

Sara glanced around, noticing for the first time how the dense foliage surrounded the gazebo like a thick web, blocking out the world. Suddenly she realized the solitude she'd always enjoyed was what made this place so dangerous.

A tight fist of fear gripped her chest. Sara forced herself to breathe and to remember she was perfectly safe. The house was close by and the security fence around the property was specifically designed to keep even the most persistent visitors out.

But zealous fans were one thing. Gary Burke was quite another. She remembered the time her mother had locked Gary out of the bedroom. Enraged, he'd kicked the door in. Her mother had paid dearly for her defiance. It had taken weeks for the bruises to fade.

Sara shuddered. If a locked door hadn't kept Gary out, how much good would a fence do?

An owl hooted in the distance and the wind rustled the leaves of the tall oak. Was that a footstep she heard? Sara's heart skipped a beat. She shoved the note back into her pocket.

Would tonight be when Gary showed up to extract his pound of flesh?

The snap of a dry branch caught her ear. Sara jerked her head in the direction of the sound. She caught a glimpse of the back half of a multicolored animal before it disappeared into the shadows.

A cat.

Sara brushed back a strand of hair with a trembling hand and smiled, feeling thoroughly ridiculous. She'd been terrified all because of the neighbor's calico?

Next time it might not be a cat.

The realization wiped the smile from her face. Next time she might not be so lucky. And she wouldn't be able to count on Crow for protection forever. Meg thought the notes had stopped. Soon her manager would have to conclude there was no reason to keep paying for a bodyguard.

"Sara?"

She jumped to her feet, her heart pounding until she saw who was in the doorway. "Crow. You scared me. What are you doing here?"

"I came to make sure that you were all right." She'd told him in no uncertain terms to stay away, yet there was not even a hint of apology in his tone. "Are you?"

His gaze bore into hers and heat rose to her face.

"I'm great." She stopped herself from adding "now that you're here," even though it was true. The fear that only moments before threatened to overtake her had vanished. Impulsively Sara patted the bench next to her. "Why don't you have a seat?"

He hesitated. "I thought you had a song to write."

She forced a laugh. "I think it needs to simmer in my head a while longer."

It was all the encouragement he seemed to need. He plopped down next to her.

Sara noticed he'd shaved since dinner, ridding his face of the five o'clock stubble that made him look so sexy. And he'd changed his clothes, replacing the khakis and polo with blue jeans and a faded University of Richmond T-shirt. She smiled. "Did you go to Richmond?"

The goal was simple—make conversation so he'd hang around.

"As a matter of fact, I did." Crow leaned back against the hard wood slats and crossed his legs at the ankles.

"I thought I detected a trace of a Southern accent," Sara teased.

"Hardly," Crow retorted, but his lips twitched.

"What was your major?" He'd always been reluctant to talk about himself and Sara knew next to nothing about his background.

Crow shifted in his seat. "Criminal justice."

Sara thought for a moment. "Ever thought about being a cop or going into law?"

"Can you see me as an attorney?" Crow

snorted. "Besides, what's wrong with what I'm doing?"

"Nothing," Sara said immediately, hoping she hadn't offended him. "But isn't it kind of tough being a bodyguard?"

"It's not that dangerous."

"I was thinking more of the insecurity of going from one job to another. Of not putting down roots anywhere."

"I guess it depends on what's important to you." He stared at her for a long moment. "What's important to you, Sara? Putting down roots?"

"Maybe."

"Let me guess," he said. "You're a woman who wants it all. The husband, two point five kids, house with a white picket fence and—"

"A collie." If he was detailing her dream life, it might as well be accurate.

"Just don't tell me you plan to call it Lassie."

"What else would I name it?"

"You're joking."

Sara lifted her chin. "I happen to love that name."

"I've got two words for you," he said. "Trite. Overdone."

"Really?" Sara raised a skeptical brow. "How many collies do you personally know named Lassie?"

He hesitated for a second, then answered grudgingly, "None."

"I rest my case," she said with a satisfied smile. "And since it's my dream, the two point five kids would be rounded up to three."

"Why not down to two?" His tone was more curious than critical.

"I love kids," she said promptly. "I want at least three."

"Three can be a bad number. There were three boys in my family and it's easy for one to feel like an outsider. You know, the old two-against-one kind of thing."

Sara remembered him talking about his brothers. Though there had been pride in his voice at their accomplishments, she'd wondered at the time if he'd been the odd man out. "I never really considered the problems with having three. Four might work."

"Or two," he added with a smile.

"I've already told you, at least three."

"Better ask James about that," Crow said with a piercing gaze.

"If I plan it right, it shouldn't interfere with my career," Sara said.

"I'm not talking about the publicity standpoint," Crow said with a strange catch in his throat. "But as the father of your babies, James might want a say in how many."

Father of your babies.

Sara squirmed, suddenly uncomfortable. It wasn't that she hadn't thought about marrying James. She had. But they'd discussed marriage in only the most abstract terms. And they'd never discussed children.

"Have I ever said I'm going to marry James?"

"No."

"That's because I don't know yet whom I'll marry." She waved a hand in the air. "Any number of men would love to marry me. I'm sure you have the same problem with women."

"I've got 'em lined up down the block," he said, playing along. "Begging, pleading with me, 'Sal marry me, please marry me.'"

Sara smiled at the blatant overdramatization, even while her thoughts lingered on his words. "Sal? It that your real name?"

Crow straightened. He hesitated as if weighing his options before answering. "Yeah, but nobody really calls me that anymore."

"Sal." She rolled the name around on her tongue and found it to her liking. "Can I call you that?"

He shrugged. "If you want to."

"Does Raven call you Sal?" She wondered why she even bothered to ask when she already had a good idea what his answer would be.

"Usually," he said. "Anyway, what does it matter what she calls me?"

But it did. Sara didn't care about dozens of women; she only cared about one. The one who seemed to know him so well, who'd called him Sal before Sara even knew that was his name.

Raven.

The one with the inside track to his heart.

Chapter Eleven

Sara rose early the next morning, her conversation with Crow still on her mind. The fact she'd just learned his real name only underscored how little she knew about the man.

Today she'd remedy that oversight. He'd asked for the day off. She'd decided to spend it with him.

It could be a battle, but Sara had come prepared. She'd left her hair down in loose waves and worn the black stretch tube dress that he'd admired soon after he started working for her. Even her makeup had gotten extra attention this morning. Though she'd never been really big on resorting to feminine wiles, Crow was a tough opponent, and difficult times called for sacrifices.

Like being up and ready to go at 6:00 a.m.

Sara knew from past experience that Crow

didn't usually leave the house before seven, but she wasn't taking any chances.

The coffeepot beeped and Sara forced herself from her chair. Hopefully the extrastrong brew would jump-start her morning. She poured herself a mugful, added a couple of sugar cubes and returned to the table to read the paper.

By the time Crow sauntered into the kitchen, looking incredibly handsome in a pair of black running pants and a T-shirt, Sara had drank three cups and was finally wide awake.

He stopped in the doorway. His gaze shifted to the clock. "What's the matter?"

"Nothing." Sara took a deep breath. She'd decided to use the direct approach. "I thought we'd spend the day together." Sara took a sip of coffee and peered at him over the rim of her cup. "Won't that be fun?"

"It could be, but it's not going to happen." Crow took the seat at the table opposite her. "My day's booked solid. I've got a bunch of errands—"

"Perfect," Sara interrupted. "I love to run errands. I can keep you company."

"Why?" he asked bluntly.

"Because I want to spend time with you."

"We're together all the time." He looked at her as if she'd gone utterly mad. "I'm your bodyguard. My job is to be with you. Remember?"

"Oh, that—" Sara waved a dismissive hand "—that doesn't count. That's work."

"And what will this be?"

From his stony expression, Sara had to admit that her plan was off to a rocky start. Impulsively she reached across the table and grabbed his hand. Surprisingly he didn't pull away.

Emboldened, she rubbed her fingers lightly across the top of his hand. "It'll be fun. C'mon, Crow. Be my friend. Let me come along. Please."

He stared for a long moment. Finally, just when she'd about given up hope, his expression softened. "Okay, you can come. But it'll be boring, not fun. Don't say I didn't warn you."

"It'll be great." Sara flashed him her brightest smile. "Just you wait and see."

It had been a good day so far, Crow conceded. All morning he and Sara had run errands; they'd gone to the bank to deposit his paycheck, returned a video, dropped off clothes at the dry cleaner's and now it was time for lunch.

He'd planned to stop by and see if his mother was free, but that would have to wait for another day. No way was he introducing Sara to his mother. In two seconds flat, Sara would know his life history. His mother never had learned how to keep her mouth shut. And his sister was cut from the same cloth. Thankfully, Sara wouldn't be crossing paths with either of them anytime soon.

"How 'bout we grab some sandwiches at the deli and head over to the zoo for a couple of hours?" Sara said with a hopeful smile.

Crow groaned to himself. His first impulse was to shoot down the idea. But she *had* been such a good sport all morning. And she did look incredibly lovely with her hair shining like spun gold and that dress showing off her curves to full advantage.

"I haven't been to the zoo in years," he said. "When I was a kid it was one of my favorite places."

"My mom and I used to go there." She paused for a moment, remembering. "We'd always eat in the Safari Café."

"I've got an idea," Crow said. "If we're going to the zoo anyway, why don't we eat at the Safari Café? You can relive those good old days."

Good old days.

Sara had never thought in those terms of the years she'd lived with her mother. But for the first time she realized that they hadn't been all bad.

Her mother may not have been the best at holding on to money or judging men, but in her own way, she'd tried to make it work. She certainly didn't deserve what she'd gotten.

"Sara? What's wrong?" Crow's voice was low and gentle. "If you want to talk about it..."

She blinked several times. Talk about it? Never. Sara shook her head and forced a smile. "I'm sorry. I guess my mind just wandered. Eating at the zoo sounds like great fun. I'm ready whenever you are."

Crow glanced at his watch as the clerk in the zoo gift shop ran up his purchase. He had less than an hour to get to the rec center.

"What did you buy?" Sara had ambled over from the other side of the store and now stood gazing curiously at the sack.

"Something for you." A Raja sweatshirt might be a rather unconventional gift, but he hoped she'd like it. After all, she'd loved the Asian elephant exhibit and had told him that Raja was her favorite.

"But I didn't buy you a gift."

"Your presence today was my gift," he said.

Sara grinned. "As if I'd believe such a corny line."

"Okay, if you want to get me something, how 'bout a new Corvette," he said promptly with a wicked grin.

Sara laughed out loud, and it only seemed natural to take her hand as they walked to the car.

Today had made him remember what it was like to be part of mainstream America. How enjoyable it was to walk on a sunny day with a beautiful woman at his side.

He couldn't help but notice the admiring glances sent her way. And the surprise on the faces of those same people when they noticed who was at her side.

Several teens recognized her and asked for an autograph. She smiled and pulled out a pen, introducing him, almost as an afterthought, as "her friend Crow." But the name that had seemed to fit for so many years sounded wrong on her lips.

They finally reached the car and he opened the door for her, reluctant to see the day end.

"I had a really nice time," Sara said, sliding onto the seat.

"Me, too," he said. Crow took his seat behind the wheel, but instead of tossing the sack into the back seat, he kept it with him.

He looked up to find Sara's gaze riveted on the sack. Though he was anxious to see her reaction, he couldn't help but worry. What if she didn't like it? Impulsively he shoved the bag at her. "Here. You might as well open it now."

She took it from him, but made no move to look inside. "This is so sweet of you."

"Just open it," he said gruffly.

She hesitated, and all of a sudden the gift seemed all wrong. Sara was a popular recording star. What would she want with an elephant sweatshirt?

He reached for the ignition.

"Let's not go yet." Her hand covered his. Her skin was warm and smooth and baby soft.

Leaving the key dangling in the ignition, Crow sat back, his insides wound as tight as a roll of barbed wire.

Sara opened the sack slowly and carefully pulled out the tissue-wrapped garment.

"I had them leave the tags on in case you want to return it."

She pushed aside the tissue and let out a little gasp. "A Raja sweatshirt." In one swift movement, Sara turned in her seat and flung her arms around his neck. "I love it. Thank you so much."

Relief flooded Crow and he let out the breath he didn't realize he'd been holding. He returned the hug, liking the feel of her hair against his face and her warm body pressed against his. He shifted slightly, reaching up with one hand to stroke her hair. It gave her ample time to pull back, but she didn't move from his arms. Instead, her gaze met his and she smiled.

It was all the encouragement he needed. He lowered his mouth to hers and kissed her like he'd wanted to since he'd first seen her this morning.

Her lips were warm and soft and she tasted like cotton candy. He nuzzled her neck. "You taste so good."

"Do I?" Sara's voice was oddly breathless. "What do I taste like?"

"Candy." He nibbled on her ear, his voice low and husky. "Sweet candy."

"Is it the kind of candy you like?"

She arched her neck and he planted kisses along her jaw.

"Mmm-hmm," he said, more than willing to show her just how sweet she was.

He kissed her again, longer this time, letting his mouth linger.

Sara's hand rose and gently caressed his cheek.

His heart raced like a Harley with its throttle wide open. He wanted nothing more than to jerk her to him and let the world explode in a blistering wave of heat and passion.

But he couldn't. Sara wasn't like other women. She was special. And that made her dangerous.

He pulled back and tried to hide his shaky breath behind a halfhearted laugh. "Wow. You really know how to turn a guy on."

A shadow of disappointment crossed her face, but he didn't have a choice. He couldn't let her see how much she meant to him. That would be awkward for both of them.

After all, he was just her employee. And like it or not, she had James. Even Crow could see they made a perfect couple. He was just a momentary diversion. As soon as he found the stalker, he'd be out of the picture. The last thing he wanted to do was to leave Sara with any regrets.

Because that wouldn't be fair to do to anyone, much less to someone you…loved.

Sara stared out the window on the drive home, her emotions as tangled as her windblown hair.

Would she ever understand him? Crow's words and actions didn't mesh. He liked kissing her—that much was obvious. But why then, just when she'd thought he was going to kiss her again, did he pull back? And what was that remark about her knowing how to turn a guy on?

A horrible thought struck her. Could he be thinking she was *too* experienced, as in *easy?*

Like mother, like daughter.

There was no truth in it. She had no intention of being intimate with anyone except her husband. The most she'd ever done was to exchange a few kisses with James and now with Crow.

But she had to admit it was a lot harder to stop at just kisses with Crow than it had been with James.

James's kisses were pleasant. Crow's kisses made her tingle all the way down to her toes. Did he worry that she wouldn't be able to call it quits?

Sara slanted a sideways glance at his stony features. It had been a beautiful day and it would be a shame to ruin it because of a misunderstanding.

"Crow, er, Sal." She shifted in her seat and cleared her throat.

He glanced at her for a brief second before turning his attention back to the road.

"Could you look at me?" she said. "I have something to say."

"In case you hadn't noticed—" his gaze flitted to her before returning on the road "—I'm driving."

Sara paused. If she waited until they got home, their conversation might be overheard. "Pull in there."

"What?"

"Pull in there." She pointed to a small roadside park off to the right.

Just when she thought he was going to ignore her and go right past, he turned in the parking lot.

He swung into a space at the very edge of the lot, shut off the car and turned to face her. "Okay, what's this about?"

His dark eyes bore into hers and she could feel her confidence slipping.

Sara took a deep breath. "Kissing."

"What are you saying? That you made me stop the car so we could kiss again?" The look in his eyes told her that though he might not fully understand the point, he'd be willing to go along with the idea.

"No. I don't want to kiss you again." Sara paused, then frowned. That hadn't come out the way she'd intended. "I mean, I *do* want to kiss you again, just not now."

He reached for the ignition. "Now that we've got that settled…"

"Let me finish." Her hand closed over his. "Please."

Crow glanced at the clock on the dash. "Will this take long?"

"I'll make it quick." Sara took a deep breath. "If you were worried when we were kissing that I wouldn't stop you from going further, you were wrong."

The beginnings of a smile tipped the corners of his mouth.

Sara could feel the heat rising up her neck, but she ignored it. She knew what she had to say and she might as well get it over with. "I have no intention of going any further with you."

His smile vanished.

"Regardless of what you may think, Sara, I'm not out to score with just anyone."

They were back on the road before she had a chance to respond.

"So, is that what I am?" she said in a soft voice. "Just anyone?"

He kept his eyes focused straight ahead and pretended he hadn't heard.

Chapter Twelve

Sara reached up and rubbed the back of her neck. It had been a long day and an even longer evening. Lately it seemed like all she'd been doing was attending parties. So why had she let James persuade her to attend yet another one?

Because he really didn't give you a choice.

With a start Sara realized it was true. James hadn't persuaded; he'd insisted. In truth she'd been so startled by his uncharacteristic demand that she'd simply agreed.

She took a sip of her sparkling water and watched James work the room. His dark suit emphasized his blond good looks and lean muscular build. He'd kept her at his side the entire evening until he'd run into an old friend from college and she'd finally managed to slip away, ostensibly to freshen up.

She'd dawdled in the elaborate washroom of the Wildwood mansion as long as she dared. She certainly didn't want James to send anyone in looking for her.

But when she'd returned to the party, James hadn't moved from where she'd left him. A third man that she vaguely recalled meeting had joined James and his friend. From their laughter, Sara concluded that for the moment the business talk had been set aside.

"Sara?"

A hand touched her shoulder from behind and she turned.

Raven smiled, looking classically elegant in a black linen sheath and pearls.

"Raven?" Sara gave her a quick hug. "What are you doing here?"

Raven waved her hand loosely in the direction of the bar. "Stephen conned me into it. How about you?"

"The same," Sara said. "James insisted I come, though I'm not sure why. He's spent the whole evening talking to everyone but me."

She didn't mean to criticize James, but the way he was constantly introducing her, then jumping right into business talk practically before she'd had a chance to say hello, had started to grate on her nerves.

"I know what you mean." Raven smiled understandingly and took a sip of her white wine. "They drag you to these things, then spend the night talking business."

"Ex-actly," Sara said. "It's crazy."

"I've often thought it would be fun to give Stephen one of those blow-up dolls and suggest he take it along to these type of functions. Then he'd have what he wanted—a beautiful woman on his arm—and I could stay home in peace."

Sara smiled and took a sip of her drink. James thought Stephen and Raven were an item. The way Raven talked, it appeared he was right.

"So," Sara said as casually as she could manage, twisting the stem of her glass between her forefinger and thumb, "do you and Stephen live together?"

"Stephen and I?" A burst of laughter erupted from Raven's throat. "Where in the world would you get an idea like that?"

A wave of heat rose up Sara's neck but she kept her gaze steady. "Well, you did say something about staying at home."

"I meant at *my* house." Raven shook her head, her smile rueful. "Stephen and I don't live together. Never have. Never will. We work together. We're good friends, but that's it."

Sara realized she must still look skeptical because Raven added, "And even if we were in love, which we aren't, I don't believe in living together before marriage."

"Really?" Sara couldn't keep the surprise from her voice. The woman before her projected a sophisticated worldly image at odds with her old-fashioned values. Like James, Sara had just assumed the two were lovers.

"Don't look so shocked." Raven's gaze was direct but her smile told Sara she hadn't taken offense. "Despite the media hype, I believe there are a lot of us out there."

"A lot of us?"

"People who believe that making love comes *after* you're married, not *before*." Raven brushed a stray strand of hair back over her shoulder. "I assume you agree?"

"Of course," Sara said. "Though I sometimes feel like I'm the only one."

"Well, there are two of us in the room tonight." Raven smiled, showing a set of white teeth as perfect as the rest of her. "And now that we've determined we're not sleeping with our boyfriends, why don't you tell me what you've been up to. Still putting up with Crow?"

"Yeah, but it hasn't been so bad. He's out with his friends tonight." Sara took a sip of her drink, finding it interesting that Raven should ask about her bodyguard.

Suddenly Sara was glad Crow had decided to take the night off and his replacement was with her instead. "I take it you haven't seen him lately?"

"No, and it makes me mad, too. I've been gone for almost a whole year and now I'm back and he never calls." Raven raised one shoulder in a careless shrug, but Sara could see the hurt in her dark eyes. "I think he's still upset I didn't come back for Christmas."

Sara took another sip of her drink and kept an interested expression on her face, hoping Raven would continue.

"I was out of the country," Raven said defensively, and Sara could tell it was a sore subject. "I tried to tell him it wasn't like I was just down the street. But he couldn't understand how I could miss Christmas with the family."

"Family?" Sara widened her gaze.

Raven stopped. She took a sip of her wine. Then another. Sara could almost see the wheels turning in her head. "I, uh, know his family pretty well." She raised the glass to her lips again, but then lowered it without drinking. "Quite well in fact. He thought it would be nice if I spent the holidays with them."

Christmas with the family.

Sara's heart sank. Their relationship had to have

been serious. Meeting the family was a big step. And it sounded like he'd brought her home often.

"It sounds like you and Crow are…close," Sara said, and smiled as if the answer didn't matter.

"Not like we used to be." A hint of sadness crossed Raven's beautiful face. "Actually, I see Nick now more than I see Crow."

As if Sara's head wasn't already swimming with names, now Raven had to introduce another to the mix. But this one was vaguely familiar. "Nick? Are you talking about Crow's brother?"

Raven's eyes widened. "You've met Nick?"

Sara shook her head slowly. "No, Crow just mentioned him once. Is he the lawyer? Or the doctor?"

"Nick's the doctor," Raven said, her voice filled with pride. "An orthopod."

Suddenly Sara understood where Raven was coming from. "So a bodyguard isn't good enough for you?" she wanted to say, but she held her tongue. After all, it wasn't her place to criticize Raven's choices. Sara had set her own sights high, too. Still, her heart ached for Crow. How hard would it be to know a woman you cared deeply for—and he did; Sara had seen it in his eyes when he'd first seen Raven in the restaurant—preferred your rich, successful brother? How that must hurt.

If he even knows.

"What does Crow think about your relationship

with Nick?'' Sara tried to keep her manner offhand and nonjudgmental.

Raven's gaze grew guarded as if she'd regretted saying so much. ''I love both of them. Crow knows that. I think it hurts him that he and I are not as close as we used to be. But at this point in our lives, Nick and I have more in common. You understand.''

Sara simply nodded, not trusting herself to speak. She'd bet her next album proceeds that Dr. Nick didn't have long hair. Or a tattoo. And she'd also bet that if the good doctor took a woman out to eat, he'd take her to Luciano's for pasta or Kincaid's for a steak rather than to a hole-in-the-wall diner for a pork tenderloin and a pitcher of beer.

But she'd also bet that Nick wasn't half the man Crow was on the inside. And Raven was a fool if she didn't realize that's what really mattered.

''Sara?'' Raven touched her shoulder. ''Are you okay? You look pale.''

''I'm fine.'' Sara shook her head and smiled ruefully. Here she was condemning Raven for pursuing the same type of man Sara had always pictured herself marrying—a Dr. Nick kind of guy; a successful professional who looked like he'd stepped off the pages of *GQ*. A James Smith kind of guy.

Her publicist met all of her qualifications. And he was a good guy, not like the type of men her mother had dated. Not like Gary Burke.

A shiver traveled up Sara's spine.

"I don't care what you say." Raven took Sara by the shoulder and propelled her to an empty table nearby. "You don't look fine."

"I'm just…hungry." Sara seized the first excuse that came to mind. And it wasn't a lie. She hadn't eaten since the morning and her stomach rumbled its displeasure.

"That I can do something about." Raven smiled. "Wait here."

In a matter of minutes, Raven returned, balancing two plates overflowing with hors d'oeuvres.

"What did you do?" Sara asked. "Clean 'em out?"

Raven's eyes crinkled and she laughed. "One guy had the nerve to say I was going to get fat."

"What did you say?" Sara picked up a tiny crab rangoon from one of the plates Raven had set on the table.

Raven reached for a water chestnut wrapped in bacon and shrugged. "Nothing. I knew he was just mad because I got the last of the caviar."

"Caviar?" Sara's gaze scanned the mounds of food. "I don't see any caviar."

Raven smiled. "That's because I ate it."

Sara chuckled and picked up an egg roll. "Sounds like something I'd have done."

If Crow wasn't in the picture, Sara had a feeling she and Raven would have become friends. It had been years since she'd had a good friend. Not since junior high. She and Deanna Jablonski had been inseparable. But once Sara went to foster care she hadn't seen or heard from Deanna.

Actually that wasn't entirely true. Last year, Deanna had sent her a letter. But after much thought and prayer Sara had chosen not to respond. Deanna was part of the past she wanted to forget even existed. Contacting her would open a door Sara was determined to keep closed.

A door Gary was equally determined to blast open.

"Does your family live in St. Louis?" Raven asked, taking a dainty bite of a chicken wing.

Sara groaned to herself. Though the question was innocent, it highlighted her main reason for keeping people at arm's length. She didn't like questions about her past and she hated to lie. "I grew up in south St. Louis. My father split when I was a baby and my mother moved away years ago."

Raven took another water chestnut from the plate and disposed of the appetizer in short order. "A woman in our office, Linda Drew, grew up in that part of town. I don't suppose you know her?"

Sara shook her head, thankful the name didn't ring any bells. But even if she'd known Raven's co-worker, she wasn't sure she'd have admitted it. "I'm afraid not."

Stuffing a tiny cracker into her mouth to forestall any further questions, Sara glanced around the room, hoping to change the topic.

James had moved closer to the bar and now stood talking to a tall broad-shouldered man with dark hair. Though she couldn't quite make out his face from this distance, he looked vaguely familiar. Sara gestured her head in James's direction. "Do you know who that guy is?"

"Which one?" Raven frowned.

"The one with the black hair, talking to James."

Raven narrowed her gaze for a moment and her expression grew thoughtful. "I think that's Jerry...oh what's his name? Birkle? Burkey? Burke? He's with..."

Sara's blood ran cold. It couldn't be him.

Gary Burke would never be at a party like this. She didn't realize she'd spoken aloud until Raven answered.

"Not Gary Burke," Raven said. "It's Jerry something. He's one of our city government officials, though right now his exact title escapes me."

Sara released the breath she'd been holding.

Raven stared at Sara. "This Gary Burke. Is he a friend of yours?"

"Friend?" Sara said in a voice that seemed to come from a long way away. "More like enemy."

Raven's gaze turned thoughtful and Sara wanted to kick herself all the way around the block. Instead, Sara forced a laugh. "I think we all have people we'd just as soon forget, don't you?"

Raven agreed and started talking about a boss she'd once had and Sara said a prayer of thanks.

Whatever had possessed her to say Gary's name? The stress of the last few months must be affecting her more than she realized. Thankfully Raven already seemed to have forgotten it. And at least she'd only said it to Raven. It could have been worse. She could have said it to Meg. Or to Crow.

"Are you about ready?" Sara's voice filtered through Crow's bedroom door. "If we don't leave soon, we're going to be late for church."

Crow grabbed his suit coat and shot a quick glance in the mirror. With his hair pulled back, and dressed in the charcoal-gray suit his parents had got him last year for Christmas, he looked... different. Not like himself.

"Crow," Impatience filled Sara's voice. "It's time to—"

He opened the door abruptly and stopped, a low whistle escaping his lips. "You look fabulous."

A smile flashed before her lips pursed. "Save the sweet talk. We're running late."

She turned on her heel, not waiting for a reply and Crow had to run to keep up with her. Before he knew it they were in the car and she was barking orders at him as if he was her chauffeur or her husband—turn left here, turn right at the light, follow the curve—until finally they reached their destination.

The church sat to the north of the parking lot on a small hill. With its white clapboard siding and arched stained glass windows, it reminded Crow of something straight out of a Thomas Kinkade painting.

He'd expected a large congregation. Instead, the building before him, with its doors open wide and a white-frocked minister at the top of the steps herding the last of the stragglers inside, couldn't have held more than a hundred people.

Crow pulled into a parking space and shut off the engine. He'd planned on being one of the crowd, an anonymous visitor. But in a church this small, there would be no place to hide. Either from the other parishioners. Or from God.

Crow reached for the door handle but Sara stopped him with a hand on his arm. Concern filled her gaze. "Is something wrong?"

"Yeah, we're going to be late if you don't get out of the car and up those steps," he growled. "C'mon, let's get this over with."

Sara slanted a sideways glance at Crow, listening to the minister's prayer with only half an ear.

Crow had his head lowered and his hands folded. If he wasn't concentrating on the pastor's words, he was a great actor. Actually, throughout the service, he'd seemed to be the one paying attention while her thoughts kept wandering.

On the way to the church, he'd told her several times how much he liked her pink dress. It was actually salmon colored but she didn't bother to correct him. She was too busy directing him to the church and admiring him.

It wasn't just the suit though; if she hadn't known his income, she'd swear the garment was hand tailored. It was his easy self-assurance, that little dimple in one cheek that flashed unexpectedly and the spicy masculine scent of his cologne.

She inhaled deeply.

"Sara." Crow's hand cupped her elbow and his voice was soft as a whisper. "Stand up."

Sara shot to her feet and warmth touched her cheeks. While she'd been mooning like some love-struck teenage girl, the prayers had ended and they'd risen for the final hymn.

Crow held out the hymnal, already open to the proper page. Her fingers closed around the book and in the process brushed against his. A spark of electricity shot up her arm.

She pretended not to notice and started in…on the wrong verse.

His lips twitched.

She jabbed him in the ribs with her elbow.

His smile widened.

She shot him a quelling glare and turned her attention to the hymnal.

The song was soon over and the minister motioned for them to sit while he read the weekly announcements. After reminding the members about the change in the choir rehearsal time and the need for extra desserts for the upcoming soup supper, Pastor Dave shifted his remarks to plans for the new sanctuary.

"Thanks to Sara Michaels's substantial gift in support of this project, I'm pleased to announce we have now reached our goal and we'll be breaking ground next spring."

Applause broke out and Sara flushed with embarrassment.

"I asked him not to say anything," Sara said to Crow.

He'd just leaned his head toward hers to hear her comment when a flashbulb exploded in front of them.

Crow reacted immediately and surged to his feet. "What the—"

She grabbed his arm and pulled him back down. "It's just Ken, the photographer for the church newsletter."

"I don't like having my picture taken," he said, his jaw setting in a stubborn tilt.

"Well, neither do I," Sara said calmly. "But there's not much we can do about it now except be *gracious.*'' She emphasized the last word so he'd be sure not to miss it.

His eyes shot ebony sparks. ''I don't like being surprised.''

''Just chill.'' Sara smiled through gritted teeth and waved at an older couple coming toward them. ''It's not a big deal. We're talking front page of a church newspaper, not the *Post-Dispatch.*''

''Good,'' he muttered.

Sara wondered why he even cared. As far as she was concerned, it wouldn't matter if the picture did make the St. Louis paper. Because the one person she'd hoped to leave in the past had already found her.

Chapter Thirteen

Sara settled back on the sofa and gazed unseeing at the sheet of music in her hand. She knew she needed to concentrate on business, but ever since Sunday, all she could think about was Crow.

After church, they'd decided to do an impromptu picnic. Returning to Sara's house, they'd packed a basketful of food, changed clothes and headed to Upland Park on the northern edge of the city.

Sitting on an old plaid blanket, they'd feasted on ham sandwiches, grapes and chips. Sara grinned, remembering his response when he'd reached for a brownie and she'd told him it would cost him a kiss. When his lips had met hers, she knew the heat coursing through her body had little to do with the bright sun overhead. And later when he'd kissed her again—just because the brownie was "extra-good"—all she could do was smile.

He liked kissing her as much as she liked kissing him. And, more importantly, she was beginning to believe that he truly cared.

That was the oddest part in this whole equation—that she should be so attracted to a man like Crow. But the more she'd thought about it, the more she'd realized that, aside from the long hair and tattoo, Crow was her type of man.

He was a Christian and he cared about others. When he let it slip that for the past two years he'd been coaching a boys' basketball team at the local Salvation Army recreation center, she realized that in his own way he'd been living his faith.

Sara dropped the sheet music to her lap. And what had she done lately to help others? When she'd dreamed of a career, she'd been filled with thoughts of proclaiming Christ's saving message with her voice and helping disadvantaged kids realize their worth and their potential. Children living the life she'd once lived.

God had blessed her many times over, allowing her to do what she loved and in the process to touch people with her music. But couldn't she be doing more?

"What's that frown about?" James breezed into the room and brushed a kiss of greeting across her cheek. He looked particularly dashing in a light gray suit with a charcoal shirt. "Bad song?"

"Song?"

James gestured to the music sheet in her lap.

"Oh, this? I've just glanced at it but I like the changes." She picked up the sheet and set it on the end table. "By the way, how'd you get in? I didn't even hear the doorbell."

"Your bodyguard let me in," James said, taking a seat next to her on the sofa. "I don't know his name. It was one of the fill-ins. Where is the main man anyway?"

"Crow?"

"No, the president," James said. "Of course, Crow."

"It's his day off." Sara shrugged. "I'm not sure where he is."

"He certainly seems to take a lot of time off," James said. "He might want to watch that."

"What do you mean?"

"I mean, the guy may soon find himself unemployed." James sounded more than a little pleased at the prospect. "Think about it for a minute. You haven't received any more notes. How much longer is Meg going to be able to justify keeping him on the payroll?"

Sara thought of the note she'd received last week. The one she'd burned yesterday. "You're right. It probably won't be much longer."

At one time she'd dreamed of having Crow gone and her life to herself. Now the thought of him leaving filled her with dread. Would she ever see him again if he left?

"And if that's not good news enough...." James reached into his briefcase and with a flourish pulled out a copy of the newspaper.

"Since when has an edition of the *Post-Dispatch* been a cause for rejoicing?" Sara said dryly.

"Since my favorite Christian singer has a full-page feature spread." His face fairly glowed. "Do you realize what this kind of publicity will do for your career?"

James was so pumped up that Sara couldn't help but share in his excitement.

She smiled, knowing what seeing this article in print meant to him. It had been a real coup, getting the newspaper to select her as the first local celebrity in their series on "hometown heroes." And he'd worked long and hard with the feature editors on the article, consulting on everything from the copy to the pictures selected.

"You deserve all the credit, James," she said, giving him a hug.

"I did it for you, Sara." His gaze met hers and the depth of emotion reflected there told her what she'd once hoped for had come true. James Smith was in love with her.

It was an odd twist of fate. He'd fallen for her just as she'd realized she loved someone else.

"James, I…" She put her hand on his arm, not wanting to ruin the moment but not wanting to lead him on, either.

"We can talk later." He blanketed her hand with his and gave it a squeeze before releasing it. "Right now, I can't wait to see how this article turned out."

"You haven't looked at it yet?" Sara couldn't believe her ears. If she'd spent all these months working on this project, she'd have been down at the distribution center at the crack of dawn, picking up the paper and reading it before she got to the car.

"No," he said. "I wanted us to read it together." He gave an embarrassed laugh and shifted his eyes from her searching gaze. "Sounds sort of corny when you say it out loud."

Her heart melted. James had always been her staunchest supporter. "I don't think it sounds corny," she said. "I think it sounds sweet."

James fumbled with the paper. "Let's see what we have here."

Sara scooted even closer and took one side of the open paper, peering with interest at the splashy article, her gaze drawn immediately to the pictures. There was one of her on stage at a recent concert, another showing her accepting the Sheldon Award and one...with her and Crow in church.

Her breath caught in her throat and she looked twice to be sure.

James gasped and she knew he'd seen it too.

"Where did that come from?" His gray eyes flashed, and for a second she thought he was accusing her of giving it to the paper rather than speaking rhetorically. "This was supposed to be a picture of you and me at that fund-raiser. How could this have happened?"

Though Sara couldn't be sure, she had an inkling of what might have occurred. Ken's cousin worked at the *Post-Dispatch*. He must have shown him the picture he'd taken for the church newsletter and the cousin evidently decided to include it in the feature.

Even to her untrained eye, she could tell the photo was something special. The late-morning light filtering in through the stained-glass windows cast a warm glow around her and Crow. It was an intimate portrait. She vaguely remembered turning toward him to say something right before Ken had snapped the picture. But she didn't recall how close his mouth was to hers. Or how his eyes glowed like dark coals. He looked incredible.

"How did they get this picture, Sara?" James asked again, more insistent this time.

Sara frowned, not appreciating his tone. Her first

instinct had been correct. He did think she had something to do with this. "How would I know?"

"That's you in the picture, isn't it?" he said. "You had to have been there when it was taken."

"Of course I was there. It was taken last Sunday right after the church service." Sara tried to keep her mounting anger under control. She told herself that James didn't realize he was acting like a jerk. "It was taken for the church newsletter. How it made the paper, I don't know."

James glanced down at the page and his mouth tightened into a thin line. She wondered what upset him more—the fact that they'd changed the layout at the last minute without checking with him, or that it was Crow in the picture with her instead of him.

If she knew James, it was probably a little of both.

"Let's see what they have to say about the two of you," he muttered. He studied the print below the picture.

"What could they say?" Sara said lightly. "They don't even know who I'm with."

"On the contrary," James said. "It seems they know everything about your bodyguard." James shifted his gaze to her. "You never told me that he's a cop on leave from the St. Louis PD."

"He's not a cop. There has to be some mistake." Sara snatched the paper from James's hand. "Let me see that."

She read quickly, a tight band gripping her chest at the words. According to the paper, Crow was really Salvadore Tucci, a detective with SLPD.

Sal. She could hear his voice. *Nobody really calls me that anymore.* And suddenly Sara knew there was no mistake.

The article went on to intimate that he and Sara had recently been seen out together and speculated that wedding bells might not be too far off.

A cop. Crow was a cop. Why would a cop take a position as a bodyguard?

I really think the police need to be involved. Meg's dogged insistence followed by her sudden acquiescence now made sense.

Sara picked up the cordless phone from the coffee table and punched in the familiar number.

"Who are you calling?" James asked.

"Meg." Anger warred with disappointment. "She's got some explaining to do."

"I'm sorry, Sara," Meg said for what had to be the tenth time. "If I'd realized you'd be so upset about this, I might not have done it."

"*Might* not have done it?" James jumped on Meg's words. "You blatantly lied to Sara, and now all you can say is you're sorry and that you *might* not do it again?"

"James." Sara cast him a quelling glance. "Not that I don't appreciate your support, but this is between Meg and me."

His face tightened as if he'd been slapped. "In that case—" he rose and his gaze shifted from Meg to Sara "—I have work to do."

Sara waited until he'd left the room before she turned back to Meg. At any other time, she would have smiled at her manager's appearance. Meg's hair was flat against her head and her only makeup was lipstick and powder. She'd obviously heard the anger in Sara's voice and had pulled on her clothes and come right over.

Meg had been more of a mother to her than her own had ever been and Sara had to steel her heart against the wave of sympathy that washed over her. She had to remember what the woman standing before her had done.

"Why did you do it, Meg?" Sara's voice broke. "I trusted you."

Meg's eyes searched Sara's. "Because I care about you. I don't want anything to happen to you. You refused to take the threat seriously. So I thought…"

"You hired a cop." Sara kept her gaze firm and direct. "When I specifically said no police."

What if Crow had found out about Gary? Her heart clenched. It would have been all over.

"What now?" Meg dropped into a chair and ran her hand through her hair like a comb.

"I'm going to get rid of Crow and get on with my life," Sara said, ignoring the ache arising from deep within that told her that although it had to be done, it wasn't going to be easy. Still, she had too much to lose to let the investigation continue.

"I thought you and Crow had become friends," Meg said. "In fact I thought maybe—"

"What?" Sara snapped.

"Maybe even more?" Meg said, lifting a brow.

"Puh-leeze," Sara said, glad her voice stayed steady. "He didn't fool me for a second. I knew he was up to something from the very beginning. I just didn't know what."

A look of disappointment flashed across Meg's face. She squared her shoulders. "What now? Are you going to get rid of me, too?"

Impulsively Sara squatted down in front of Meg and took her hands. "You're my manager and my friend. I realize that what you did, you did out of concern."

"I *was* worried. I never wanted to lie—"

"Meg," Sara interrupted, not interested in her manager's excuses. "There's just one thing."

"What is that?"

"Don't do it again." Sara shot Meg a leveling gaze. "Don't lie to me, either. Because even though I care about you, I won't have people around that I can't trust.''

Crow knew something was wrong the minute he walked through Sara's front door. The replacement guard was nowhere to be found and the house, normally filled with activity, was strangely silent.

Trying to still his rising panic, Crow moved quickly through the house, searching each room. He found Sara in the den, sitting on the couch, staring into an unlit fireplace, her feet pulled up beneath her.

He released the breath he didn't realize he'd been holding. ''There you are. I've been looking all over for you.''

''Have a seat.'' Sara picked up the newspaper that had been lying open on her lap. ''We need to talk.''

''We sure do.'' He dropped into the chair opposite her. ''What happened to Larry?''

''I let him go,'' she said, her expression flat and unreadable.

An uneasy sensation of foreboding coursed through his veins.

''Was he sick?'' Of course even if he was, that was no excuse for leaving Sara unattended. Larry had his cell number. He could have called. What if something had happened to Sara? His chest tightened at the thought. "Why did he leave you alone?"

"I fired him." Sara's gaze met his and her blue eyes were ice cold. "And now I'm firing you."

"What are you talking about?" His brows drew together in a puzzled frown.

"You're fired," she said tersely. "Get your stuff and get out."

"I'm not going anywhere until you tell me what's going on." He leaned back and deliberately crossed his arms.

"Oh, you'll be leaving all right. Even if I have to call one of your fellow officers down at the police department and have them escort you out."

"So you know," he said. He wondered why he wasn't more surprised. "How did you find out?"

Sara didn't answer. She just stared at him.

"It doesn't matter. Let me explain—"

"Explain what?" She jerked to her feet and crossed the room. "That you lied to me? That you took this job under false pretenses? That you pretended to care for me just to further your investigation?"

He'd come to know her so well that he could see the pain behind her words, and compassion filled him. This was not the way he'd wanted her to find out his true identity. He'd never wanted to hurt her. "Sara…"

"I don't want your excuses." She strode to the door. "I want you to leave."

It didn't surprise him that she was angry. He'd never liked being lied to, either. In fact, just this morning he'd been thinking of telling her who he really was and why Meg had hired him. Now someone had beat him to it.

"Tell me one thing." He sat back in the chair, making no move to leave. "How did you find out?"

"I read it in the paper," she said sarcastically.

"C'mon, be serious," he said, keeping his tone conversational despite Sara's fierce glare. "How'd you find out?"

"What does it matter?" she said. "I know I want you to leave."

"Sara, be reasonable," he said. "You need protection. I've seen it before. Stalkers can and do kill."

"Well, I guess I'll just have to be careful, won't I?" Sara's voice dripped with sarcasm.

"You're a fool if you think you can do this alone." Crow shook his head in disgust and rose from the chair. He crossed the room in long deliberate strides and stopped directly in front of her. "You need me."

"That's where you're wrong." Sara stared at him unblinkingly. "I don't need anyone. Least of all you."

Chapter Fourteen

Regardless of what Sara believed, the woman needed help and Crow was going to be there for her. He was going to find the guy that was stalking her, whether she wanted him to or not. Whether she helped him or not.

Crow stared at the magazines and newspapers stacked on the floor. Since he had so little to go on, he'd decided to start at the beginning of Sara's career and see if he could find some clue there.

He'd just finished going through one stack of magazines when the doorbell rang. Crow hesitated, debating whether or not to answer it.

"It's me." His sister's voice traveled through the flimsy wood. "And I saw your cycle out back so don't even try to pretend you're not home."

Crow heaved a resigned sigh. He stepped over

the pile of papers and unlocked the door. "C'mon in. Watch your step."

Raven halted abruptly and glanced around the room. She'd never pulled any punches about her feelings regarding his studio apartment on Compton Street. Not only didn't she like the area, she thought the place was way too small. Right now, seeing it through her eyes, he had to agree.

"Don't tell me. You've decided to supplement your income by recycling."

"I'm in the middle of doing some research." He offered her his hand and she stepped across the piles and took a seat in an empty spot on the couch.

She wrinkled her nose. "When are you going to move out of this dump and get yourself a decent place? Mom was telling me about this cute house in Hazelwood that's a real steal. I could get some details if you're interested."

"Don't bother." Her hopeful expression faded with his words. "This place is all I need. I'm gone all the time anyway."

It was the same answer he'd been giving her and the rest of his family since he'd moved into this place south of downtown two years earlier. "In fact, my lease is up next month and I plan to sign on that dotted line as soon as I get the contract."

"I'd think carefully before I'd do that." Raven smiled. "It might be big enough for one, but it's certainly not large enough for two."

"Two?" Crow frowned. "What are you talking about?"

"No need to play the confirmed bachelor with me. It's not a secret anymore, bro." Raven's eyes danced with amusement. "Mom called me this morning right after she'd read the paper, wanting the scoop. She'd have called you but she says you never tell her anything."

"What are you talking about?" A cold knot formed in his stomach.

"As if you don't know. The article in the paper?" Raven teased. "The one that predicts wedding bells for you and Sara?"

Raven pulled a newspaper out of her oversize purse and handed it to him. "I brought you an extra copy."

I read it in the paper.

His heart clenched. "Does the article give my name and say that I'm a cop?"

"You know it does." Raven stared at him curiously. "I hope you finally told Sara I was your sister and that you'd sworn me to secrecy. I wouldn't want her to be mad."

"Oh, she's not mad." She's furious.

"Good." Raven brushed a kiss across his cheek. "Cuz when you two get married, I'd like to be a bridesmaid."

Before he could think of an appropriate response, she'd risen, stepped back over the piles and opened the door. "I've got to run. Good luck on your research."

He lifted a hand in a halfhearted goodbye. The door closed and he sank back on the couch, rubbing a hand across his forehead.

Ever since he'd left Sara's house, he'd told himself that she was just upset, but that she'd get over it. Now he wasn't so sure.

If he tried to go the apology route, he knew she'd want him to promise to drop the investigation. And he couldn't do that. Not when her life might be at stake.

All he could do was believe that, no matter how hurt or angry she was, one day she'd understand there are some things you just have to do. And then she'd forgive him.

At least he hoped so. Because if she didn't forgive him, chances were she wouldn't marry him, either.

Sara pushed the rest of her entrée to the side of her plate. She loved salmon but she hadn't had much of an appetite lately. For James's sake she'd tried to put on a good show, eating at least a bite or two of everything on her plate.

James had chosen Hannegan's for a celebratory dinner. Not only had her latest release been a great seller in the Christian market, it was doing surprisingly well on the pop charts, as well.

"Is something wrong with the salmon?" James frowned and looked around for the waiter. "I'll have them get you something else."

"Please don't." Sara placed a restraining hand on his arm. "It's delicious. I'm just not that hungry."

"Tell me this isn't about some crazy diet." James's gaze turned sharp and assessing. "Because, if anything, you could stand to put on a few pounds."

"No, really." She laughed. Who but a man would encourage a woman to *gain* weight? "I'm just full."

"If you're sure…"

"I'm positive." Sara glanced around the interior of the restaurant. Hannegan's casual elegance and unique political décor set it apart from the other eateries in the Laclede's Landing area. For years it had been one of her favorite places to eat. "Dinner was great. And you know how much I like jazz."

"That's why I picked this place." James's expression grew smug. "I wanted it to be special."

"It has been," Sara said, wishing in that instant that everything could be the way it used to be between her and James. But no matter how much she tried to pretend, the feelings weren't there. Oh, she cared about James. She admired him. But love? No, she didn't love him. She couldn't love him. Her heart already belonged to someone else.

Dear God, with all the men in the world, just tell me one thing—why Crow?

Crow rubbed a weary hand across his forehead and leaned back in the chair, the newspaper on his lap falling to the cluttered floor. He kicked it off to the side with his foot.

All the articles on Sara and her career had started to run together. Though the spin on each might be different, the basic information was the same. After three days of reading, he was no closer to finding out who was stalking her.

A sick feeling filled the pit of his stomach every time he thought about Sara being unprotected. Without him around, she was a sitting duck.

Crow had never been a vengeful man. But he knew if someone hurt Sara, they would pay. He'd personally see to it. Though he still couldn't understand why anyone would want to harm her. She was a good person who had worked hard for her success. He'd found no indication that she stepped on anyone along the way. And knowing Sara, if she had, it would have been accidental rather than intentional.

She didn't have a mean bone in her body, though she had plenty of stubborn ones. Crow had run smack-dab into that irritating characteristic when he'd called her to clear the air.

The first time he'd called, Annie had answered

and told him Sara was unavailable but that she would give Sara his message. He'd waited a few days then called again. The next time Sara had picked up the phone herself. She'd promptly hung up when she heard his voice. He hadn't called since.

Salvadore Tucci didn't grovel for any woman. No matter how much he loved her.

He shook his head, unable to believe the strange twist of fate. She'd changed his life and now she didn't want him.

Thanks to his time with Sara, he'd finally realized something his family had been trying to tell him all along—that he wasn't Crow, a guy who talked like a junkie or drug dealer and who was cynical and suspicious and cared only for himself. He was still Sal, the guy who went into law enforcement believing he could make a difference.

He had only a few weeks left of his leave. Then he'd have to tell the chief whether or not he was coming back to the force. It would be a difficult decision. But he'd decided to do what he should have been doing all along with major decisions; he was going straight to the top.

He'd started praying for guidance. Every night before he closed his eyes he'd ask the Almighty for direction. But while he waited for an answer, there was work to do. Crow glanced at the stacks. With a resigned sigh, he reached over and grabbed a magazine from the top of the next pile, one promising a "tell-all" story about Christian singer Sara Michaels.

As he flipped to the page, he prayed that this wouldn't end up being another article geared to teens. One that gave the inside scoop on what kind of deodorant Sara loved, her favorite perfume for a night on the town and how she kept her hair so soft and shiny. He'd read enough of those to last a lifetime.

He scanned the article, written last year by a freelance journalist out of St. Louis. This woman had clearly done her research. The mention of Sara's mother having a series of live-in boyfriends was a new revelation. But it was the quotes attributed to one of Sara's junior high classmates that caught his eye. Though the woman didn't go into detail, what she did say showed she didn't hold her old friend in very high regard. "I don't think her fans would still love her if they knew the real Sara Michaels."

What had that one note said? The one that had caught his eye because the paper and lettering had been different than the others? "Would your fans still love you if they knew you were a thief?"

The wording was too similar to be coincidental. Crow's heart rate surged like it did when a big bust was going down. He reached for the phone and quickly dialed a friend at the police station. Joe would know the fastest way to reach this journalist and in turn the journalist would lead him to this—he glanced down at the article—Deanna Jablonski.

Crow didn't even curse when he was put on hold. He had a solid lead. Nothing else mattered.

Chapter Fifteen

An old Ford Escort sat in the driveway of the south St. Louis bungalow and Crow could hear the television blaring inside. He pulled the piece of paper from his pocket and glanced at the address one last time, wanting to be sure he had the right place before he knocked.

It had been surprisingly easy to track down Deanna Jablonski. She was a lifelong St. Louis resident and this little house wasn't far from where she and Sara had grown up.

Crow rapped on the door and waited. He waited a minute then knocked again, a little louder this time.

He smiled at the security system decal on the weathered storm door. Crow knew people of all income levels often put up such signs believing they acted as a deterrent. Unfortunately in this neighborhood, Ms. Jablonski would have been smarter to invest in a good dead bolt lock.

He shifted and hit the door two more times with the back of his fist. Hard.

"I'm coming. Just give me a minute," a feminine voice from inside yelled.

He smiled and lifted his gaze. Today *was* his lucky day.

An unfamiliar reflection stared back from the smudged glass of the door. The hair that had once trailed down his back now barely brushed his shoulders. He'd gone in, fully intending to get it cut short but at the last minute he'd changed his mind and only four inches had fallen to the floor.

"May I help you?" A woman's fleshy face surrounded by a mass of tightly permed curls peered around the door.

"Deanna Jablonski?" Crow asked.

"Maybe." Suspicion clouded her eyes. "Who wants to know?"

"Detective Tucci, St. Louis PD." He reached into his pocket for his wallet, opening it to his picture ID and his badge. "I'd like to ask you a few questions."

"You don't look like a cop."

He groaned to himself but kept a smile on his face. "You can call the station if you want."

"Am I in tr-trouble?" she stammered. "I know

I paid that parking ticket late, but I did pay it. I think I even have a copy of the—''

''Ma'am.'' Crow stopped her before she could shut the door and go in search of her canceled check. ''It's not about the parking ticket. May I come in? Or do you want to talk here on the porch?''

She hesitated. Her gaze slid back to the identification and badge he still held open in his hand.

''I guess you can come inside.'' She released the chain and held open the door. ''Excuse the mess. I've been cleaning.''

Crow had been in many houses just like hers over the years and he prepared himself for unending clutter and overflowing ashtrays. To his surprise, not only was the place neat as a pin, it smelled like freshly baked apple pie.

The only clue that she'd been cleaning was a can of furniture polish and a dust rag on top of the end table and a vacuum with its cord still plugged in sitting off to one side.

''Can I get you something to drink?'' Her hands fluttered nervously. ''I have iced tea or lemonade.''

''No, thank you.'' Crow took a seat on a green plaid couch and pulled a notepad out of his back pocket. ''But I can wait while you get yourself some.''

''I'm fine.'' She moved to a nearby wooden rocker and sat down, ignoring the folded afghan draped over the seat. "I just want to know what this is all about."

She brushed a strand of hair back from her forehead, her expression clearly worried. The tiny lines around her eyes and her callused hands showed she hadn't had an easy life, yet on first impression she didn't seem mean or vindictive. What would have made her turn on an old friend? It couldn't have been money. The journalist hadn't paid any of his sources.

"Ms. Jablonski—"

"Please call me Dee," she said. "Everybody does."

"Is that what Sara Michaels called you?"

"What does she have to do with anything?" The polite smile slipped from her face.

"I read the interview you did last year."

"It's a free country." She lifted her chin. "And everything I said was the truth. If she said any different—"

"What happened between you and Ms. Michaels?" Crow said in a low smooth voice. "It sounded like you two used to be close friends."

"We were." Dee twisted a piece of the afghan between her thumb and forefinger. "But since she's gotten to be such a star, she doesn't have time for her old friends."

"Is that so?" he said.

She lifted her gaze and he could see the hurt in

her eyes. "Sara and I weren't just good friends, we were best friends. We told each other everything. You'd think that would mean something to her."

"You sound bitter."

"I don't really care anymore," she said. "I just don't like reading how wonderful she is, like she's some sort of saint or something. If her fans knew what she was really like, they wouldn't think she was so great."

Crow's breath caught in his throat. There it was again. The same basic message that had been present in the note Sara had received. He lifted a questioning brow. "Are you aware that Ms. Michaels had recently received a threatening note with that same sentiment?"

The color drained from her face and Crow knew he'd hit pay dirt.

"Why did you send the note, Dee?" Crow said softly.

"Who said I sent it?" The woman's tone was surprisingly casual but little beads of sweat dotted her forehead.

"You asked why I was here," he said. "Did you know that with today's technology we can get a fingerprint off an envelope and tie it to the person who sent it?"

Crow wasn't lying. You *could* isolate a fingerprint off of an envelope. Unfortunately, not off the one she'd sent.

She lifted her gaze. Instead of being contrite, her eyes flashed. "Okay. Big deal. I sent one lousy note. And, just for the record, I didn't threaten her."

"Why did you send it?" He repeated the question she'd still not answered.

"Did she tell you I called her last year?"

He shook his head.

"I'm not surprised," she said. "I thought it might be nice if we'd get together. Talk about old times."

"And?" he prompted.

"She never called back." Dee emphasized every word and the hurt mixed with the anger in her eyes.

"Did you ever think she might not have gotten your message?" He couldn't imagine Sara deliberately dissing her old friend.

"Oh, she got it," Dee said, her lips tightening into a thin line. "I didn't just call once. I'd left at least two or three messages on her voice mail before I finally got her manager. I think her name was Mary."

"Meg," Crow murmured, but Dee didn't seem to hear.

"She told me Sara had gotten my messages and that she was very busy, but that she'd have her call me." Dee stared at Crow. "She never did."

Crow frowned. "That doesn't sound like Sara."

"At least not the Sara you read about in the

paper." Dee shook her head. "But nobody's that good. Not even someone that sings like an angel."

"Lots of people seem to think Sara Michaels is practically perfect," he said, his words a deliberate attempt to provoke a response.

"That's a good one." Dee's laughter had a sharp edge. "Sara? Someone who didn't think twice about stealing?"

"What are you talking about?" Crow couldn't keep the surprise from his voice. "Who did she steal from?"

Dee started to speak, then stopped. Her expression grew guarded. "Forget I said anything. I gotta learn to keep my mouth shut. My pastor tells me if I can't say something nice, I shouldn't say anything at all."

Though normally Crow would have agreed with her minister, in this instance he wished she'd have waited a little longer to decide to follow the man's advice.

Crow thought quickly and shifted gears. "Let me ask you another question. This one doesn't have anything to do with being nice or not. Do you have any idea why Sara's mother put her in foster care?"

"I don't really know." Dee lifted one shoulder in a slight shrug. "One day she was in school. The next day she was gone."

"Didn't you ask her mother where she was?"

"I couldn't," Dee said. "She was in the hospital. Her boyfriend had gone crazy, beat her half to death." Dee shook her head. "Sara and I always knew he was bad news. The guy was a real perv. And a mean one, to boot."

Crow's jaw tightened. He'd seen more than his share of such men in his years on the force. "And you haven't seen Sara or her mom since?"

"I haven't seen Sara," Dee said. "But her mother works as a waitress in a little diner over on Pine. I run into her occasionally."

Crow took down the name and address of the restaurant, though he wasn't sure why. He'd solved the case. Sara was safe. Dee had never meant to harm her.

But talking with Dee had raised some questions. Questions that weren't part of the investigation but ones he was nonetheless determined to answer.

His gaze lowered to the address in his hand. He was suddenly in the mood for food and conversation. This might be a good time to try one of the restaurants on Pine.

Crow waited until one-thirty to head over to Pine Street. By the time he walked through the door, there were only two tables of customers lingering over coffee and dessert.

Small and quaint, the place held less than fifty when full. Crow quickly scanned the interior, noting a dark-haired man back in the kitchen area and a woman who looked to be in her forties wiping off a table.

He stared for a moment wondering if this could be Sara's mother. She was a bit young but her coloring matched.

"Ma'am." He cleared his throat.

"Oh, I'm sorry." She quickly crossed the room and grabbed a menu. "I didn't see you. Table for one?"

Crow nodded and followed her to a booth by the window.

"Can I get you something to drink while you look at the menu?"

"Actually—" Crow hesitated and glanced at the woman's name tag "—Ilene, I was wondering if I could talk to you a minute? It's about your daughter, Sara."

Her blue eyes widened and in that moment she looked so much like Sara, he knew he'd been right to take a chance. This had to be her mother.

"I have a few questions—"

"First I have a few questions of my own." Ilene eyed him with a calculating expression. "Who are you? And what do you want from me?"

In answer he pulled out his picture ID and badge and laid them on the table in front of her. "I'm a police officer. And, like I said, I just want to ask you some questions. It shouldn't take long."

Her face paled and she glanced at the cash register. The dark-haired guy from the kitchen was ringing up the last of the customers.

"John, I think I'll take my break now," she said.

"No problem." His curious gaze shifted from her to Crow. "I'll be in the back if you need me."

Ilene slid into the booth opposite Crow.

Now that he had her attention, Crow couldn't seem to find the words. How do you ask a woman how she could go for ten years without speaking to her own daughter? Even he talked to his own mother at least once a week.

"You said this was about Sara." Ilene's voice cracked and worry furrowed her brow. "Is she in trouble?"

"She's fine," he said. "But she's recently received some threatening notes and that investigation led me to you."

"You think *I* sent them?" Her hand rose to her throat.

"No," Crow said immediately. His conscience told him he should tell her he'd already found the perpetrator but he still had questions that needed answers. "But in researching Sara's past, some things are unclear and they may be relevant to the investigation. I understand Sara lived with you and your boyfriend until she was fifteen."

Ilene's gaze dropped to the table. She nodded. "Gary had moved in with us when Sara was thirteen or so. Why I stayed with that man for so long I couldn't say. Sara was right from the beginning. He was no good.''

''Where is he now?'' Crow said in a tone designed to keep the conversation flowing.

''In prison, last I knew.''

''Why did Sara go into foster care?'' Crow asked.

Ilene hesitated so long, he'd wondered if she'd heard the question. When she finally spoke, she kept her voice to a whisper even though they were alone in the dining area. ''Promise me this will be kept confidential.''

Crow nodded. ''You have my word.''

''I'll hold you to that promise.'' Ilene met Crow's gaze head-on and he could see some of her daughter's determination in her eyes. ''Gary Burke was a hard-drinking man with a hair-trigger temper. But he could be good, even sweet. For a long time I thought I was in love with him. Sara...well, Sara hated him.''

Sympathy welled up in Crow, thinking of a young girl growing up in such a home. How different his childhood had been. He'd grown up with two parents who loved each other. And him. He'd taken it all for granted. ''What happened?''

''Things had been getting worse between me and Gary. There was a guy I worked with. His name was Mike,'' she said with an embarrassed laugh. "He treated me like a queen. One day I decided I'd had it with Gary. We'd gone out drinking the night before and he'd been hitting on all these women. The next morning I told him to get out. That I'd found someone else who appreciated me."

She paused and Crow impatiently waited for her to continue.

"Gary beat me up. He'd done it before but this time he almost killed me." Though tears glistened in her eyes her voice was as matter of fact as if she was reciting the day's menu selections. "I spent five days in ICU, two weeks in the hospital. When I got out, I moved in with Mike. But he didn't like kids, and I was in no shape to take care of Sara. I could barely get around. So—"

"You put her in foster care."

"She'd been there since I went into the hospital. And she was doing okay. That's what the social worker told me."

"You left her there." Crow didn't even try to hide the condemnation in his voice.

"Don't you think I regret it?" she said. "But by the time Mike and I split, Sara had been in the same home for over a year. I decided she was better off with them than with me."

He knew he should say something about understanding how hard it must have been, but he couldn't choke out the lie.

"Sara always wanted a different kind of life than I could give her." Ilene lifted her gaze defensively. "This gave her that chance."

Incredulous, Crow could only stare.

"Look, you don't know me or my situation." Her eyes flashed. "I've made mistakes and I'm sorry for them. God has forgiven me even if Sara never has."

"Have you ever asked for her forgiveness?" he said.

"I haven't seen her since she was fifteen." Ilene traced an imaginary pattern on the linen tablecloth.

"What if she wanted to get together?" he asked. "Would you go?"

A glimmer of hope flashed in her eyes. "Does she really want to see me?"

"I believe she does," he said slowly. Sara needed to set things right with her mother. Seeing her again would be the first step. "It would be good for both of you."

Ilene's gaze flickered over Crow. "You care about my daughter."

Crow shrugged. "It's hard not to care about Sara."

"I bet she likes you, too." Ilene smiled.

"She hates my hair," he said without thinking.

"I'm not surprised." Her mother chuckled. "Gary had hair like yours. He was a jerk, but I tried to tell her that just because someone has a ponytail and a couple of tattoos doesn't mean they're not a quality kind of guy."

On a purely philosophical basis, Crow agreed with her. After all, he'd given that very same response when his parents had commented on his appearance. But lately he'd wondered if the way he looked might not be standing in the way of others seeing the real him.

"I like you," she said. "Do me a favor, will you? Take care of my daughter. Don't let anything happen to her."

"You have my word," Crow said. "No one is going to hurt Sara. Not as long as I'm around."

After leaving the café, Crow headed straight to Sara's house. He still didn't understand Dee's comment about stealing, but after less than an hour with her mother, he knew Sara's life hadn't been easy. And he didn't know one person who hadn't done something they'd regretted. He was just glad to find out there was no stalker.

Sara had been right. Meg *had* overreacted. After all, the messages in the notes, although worrisome, hadn't been overtly threatening. But Sara was bound to be happy it was all over. And he wanted to be the one to tell her.

Crow reached the edge of Sara's property and pulled up to the touch pad that controlled the security gate. He punched in five numbers and held his breath, hoping she hadn't changed the code. A green light flashed on the display panel and the gate swung open.

Crow put the car into gear and quickly drove through. It didn't take long to reach the house. He parked and wondered if it would be pushing his luck to use the house key he'd conveniently forgotten to return.

His hand stilled on the key ring. But common sense won out over temptation and he dropped the ring of keys into his pants pocket.

His hand rose to knock just as the door flew open.

"Crow." Annie's eyes widened and she stopped abruptly, her hand reaching to the doorframe for support. "I didn't expect to see you again."

"I need to talk to Sara," he said. "Is she in?"

"I'm not sure." Annie hesitated and glanced back into the house.

He smiled and brushed past Annie. "I'll show myself in."

"Annie, who was at—" Sara came around the corner.

She stared. He'd come back. She'd kicked him out, but he couldn't stay away. For an instant, pure joy raced through her body. It had been a week since she'd seen him. It seemed like a lifetime.

He looked good. Real good. So good, she wanted nothing more than to throw herself into his arms. But at the last minute she remembered what he'd done. How he'd lied to her. Used her.

Sara took a step back and crossed her arms. "What are you doing here?"

Rather than putting him in his place, her high-handed tone seemed to amuse him. His smile widened. "I came to see you."

"Sara?" Annie spoke from the doorway, her gaze shifting from Sara to Crow. "Is there anything you need me to do?"

Sara's heart warmed at the concern in her housekeeper's voice. Regardless of how attracted Annie was to the man, it was obvious her loyalties lay with Sara.

"No, you go on to the store. I'll be fine."

Not until Annie pulled the door shut behind her did Sara's gaze return to Crow. For a brief moment when his dark eyes met hers, she let herself fantasize that he'd come to apologize, to beg for her forgiveness and to tell her he'd dropped the investigation.

"I know who wrote the notes," he said, apparently deciding to bypass the social niceties.

"Really?" Her blood ran cold, but she forced herself to remain calm. He hadn't found Gary. If he had, she would have seen it in his eyes. But there was no disappointment or condemnation reflected in his charcoal depths. Sara wasn't sure what game he was playing, but for now she'd play along. "And here I thought I'd specifically told you to stay out of my business."

His brows drew together. "Did you hear what I just said?"

"I'm not deaf. Of course I heard what you said." She motioned for him to follow her into the living room, giving her heart rate a chance to slow. "Problem is I don't believe you."

"Then why am I here?"

She remembered her first thought. It made sense, but what if her intuition was wrong? She shoved her reservations aside. What other reason could there be? "You want things to be back the way they used to be between us."

"Is that so?"

Her confidence faltered but she took a deep breath and continued. "You decided you needed a reason to stop by, so you decided to tell me you'd found the stalker."

"Sounds like you've got it all figured out."

"I'm right, aren't I?" she said with more confidence than she felt.

He studied her thoughtfully. "You didn't return my calls. When I did reach you, you hung up on me." He raised a dark brow. "And yet you really think I'd come here and what? Beg you to forgive me for doing my job? For doing what I was hired by your manager to do?"

"Crow, I..."

He shook his head. "You're the one who needs to apologize. Talk about overreacting."

"Don't you put this on me," she said, anger replacing her embarrassment. Goodness knows she'd seen the guys her mother had lived with play this game often enough. Turning the tables, trying to make the innocent one feel guilty. Well, it may have worked with her mother but it wasn't going to work with her. "I know how guys like you operate. What's that old saying? The best defense is a good offe—"

"Guys like me?" A steely edge she hadn't heard before ran through his voice and there was no humor in his laughter. "I'm glad to know you hold me in such high regard."

"Sal, I didn't mean—"

"Call me Crow. After all, that's who I am to you. A long-haired guy with a tattoo. That's all you've ever seen when you've looked at me."

"That's not true."

"Isn't it?" he said. "I come to tell you I've found your stalker, and you don't even believe me."

She wanted to say she believed him, but she couldn't. Not when she knew it wasn't the truth.

"Deanna Jablonski wrote the notes," Crow said flatly. "She was angry with you for ignoring her calls but she never meant any harm. In fact, she'd still like to hear from you. Here." He handed her a sheet of paper with two names and phone numbers written in bold black print.

"Deanna?" Sara was too surprised to even glance down. "She wrote the notes? Are you sure?"

"She confessed."

Her body sagged with relief. Gary hadn't come back after all. She'd worried for nothing. Her gaze drifted to the paper in her hand. Sara frowned. "What is my mother's name doing on this?"

"I talked to her today," he said.

She spoke with a deceptive calmness. "About what?"

"About you," he said. "About what happened before you went into foster care. And about some guy named Gary Burke."

Chapter Sixteen

The blood in Sara's veins turned to ice. Her heart pounded so hard she could barely breathe, much less talk. Still, she had to say something.

"What about Gary Burke?" she finally choked out.

Crow's brows drew together, his expression sharp and assessing.

Sara stifled a groan. Why hadn't she kept her mouth shut? He'd clearly expected her to ask about her mother but like a fool, she'd focused on Gary. She took a seat in a nearby chair and tried to act nonchalant. "I mean, he and my mother aren't still together, are they?"

"No." Crow took a seat on a nearby couch. "She said he's in prison."

Sara released the breath she'd been holding. *Praise the Lord.*

"I still can't believe Dee wrote the notes," she murmured, unable to understand how the girl who'd been such a good friend and confidante could have done such a thing.

"She said she did it to get back at you for not returning her calls."

"Seems a bit extreme," Sara said dryly. "But I'm just glad it's finally over."

They sat there in silence for a long moment until Crow spoke. "You know, I spoke to your mother. Aren't you going to ask about her?"

Sara lowered her gaze, not wanting Crow to see her uncertainty. "How is she?"

"She's a beautiful woman," he said. "I was surprised at how much you two look alike."

They always had. She remembered when she'd started junior high and everyone thought they were sisters, rather than mother and daughter. Her mother would roll her eyes and they'd both giggle.

Sara's heart clenched. "Yeah, well…"

"She'd like to see you."

"I'll bet," Sara said, not bothering to hide her sarcasm.

"I'm just telling you what she told me," he said with a shrug. "I think not seeing you has been hard on her. I got the distinct feeling she's been carrying around a ton of guilt."

"Guilt?" She'd imagined her mother feeling a lot of things over the years but guilt wasn't one of them. That was Sara's cross to bear. "What does she have to feel guilty about?"

"How about for leaving you in foster care?" Crow stared as if she'd suddenly lost her mind. "For never coming back to get you?"

"I understood," Sara said. And she did. Her selfish action had almost cost her mother her life. Why *would* anyone want a daughter like that? "Anyway, it was no big deal. My foster parents were great."

"That's what your mother said. She thought they'd be able to give you the kind of life you wanted, the life you deserved."

"She said that?" Sara shot him a skeptical look, but surprisingly he appeared sincere.

Crow nodded and gestured to the paper she still held in her hand. "I put her phone number on that sheet. Are you going to call her?"

"I'm not sure. I have to think about it." She crumpled the piece of paper between her fingers but kept it in her hand. "You said she talked about what happened before I went into foster care. What did she say?"

Crow shifted uneasily in his seat. "She said she and...? What was his name? The one we were just talking about. Her boyfriend at the time?"

"Gary," Sara said, her voice strangled.

"That's right," he said. "Anyway, she said they hadn't been getting along, but you probably knew that."

Sara gave a noncommittal nod. "Go on."

"Basically she said they'd been out partying and he was all over these other women. She said she'd finally had enough. The next morning she told him she had a new guy and that she wanted Gary gone. Gary showed her with his fists what he thought of *that* idea."

Sara had seen firsthand the aftermath of that encounter. The picture of the blood-drenched carpet and upturned furniture that had greeted her when she'd arrived home was still vivid in her mind. The Social Services worker that met her at the door had assured her that her mother would be fine and that the doctors at the hospital were giving her mother the best of care. But even at fifteen, Sara had been nobody's fool. From the way the place had looked, she'd known her mother was in bad shape.

Sara's stomach churned and it took all she had to shove the memories aside. She took a deep breath, steadying herself. He'd obviously saved the worst for last.

"And the money?" Sara said. "What did she say about that?"

Crow frowned. He'd told her everything he knew. Money hadn't even been mentioned, except in a roundabout way. "Not much, except maybe how hard it would have been for her to make it on her own.''

"That's all?'' Sara demanded. "She didn't say anything about some missing money?''

Missing money? Crow paused and thought for a moment.

"The only one that had anything to say about that was Dee.'' Though Dee hadn't exactly specified *what* had been stolen, Crow followed his gut feeling and took a chance. "She said something about you stealing money?''

He riveted his gaze on Sara and waited for her reaction.

Sara blanched. "She did?''

He pressed his luck. "She told me all about it. But I'd like to hear your side.''

Sara rested her head against the back of the chair and briefly closed her eyes. "So you know.''

Crow's heart twisted at the despair in her tone, and despite his earlier anger, he wanted nothing more than to take her in his arms and comfort her. But if he did she might continue to keep whatever this secret was locked inside. And he had the distinct feeling this was something that had already festered too long.

"I'd like to hear your side,'' he repeated softly.

"There was no excuse for what I did.'' Sara's gaze was direct and firm but her eyes glistened in the light.

"Tell me." Crow offered an encouraging smile and leaned forward, resting his arms on his thighs.

She shifted her gaze to a point over his left shoulder. "My mom had never been good with money. There were always guys moving in and out and she refused to charge them so much as a dime for rent or food or anything. Then one day the money ran out. We lost the apartment and ended up on the street."

"It must have been hard." He'd worked a beat in south St. Louis for several years before he made detective and Crow had seen his share of people in such situations. Unlike some of his colleagues he'd never hardened to the plight of the homeless, especially the children.

"It was horrible. I vowed that I was never going to live out of a doorway or a car ever again." Determination ran like a steel thread through her words. "Once we were able to get a place, I decided if my mom didn't have the guts to charge her 'friends,' I would. I figured out what I thought would be a fair amount, and whenever I got the chance I'd take it from their wallets—ten or twenty dollars at a time."

He kept his face expressionless, knowing she needed him to listen more than she needed an outpouring of sympathy.

"I suppose you think I'm terrible." Her voice was heavy with self-condemnation.

"I think you were a little girl who did what you thought you had to do."

"God says 'Thou shalt not steal.'" Her blue eyes had never looked so big or so luminous. "You said before that stealing wasn't justified."

"I'm not anyone's judge and jury, Sara," he said. "You were worried about keeping a roof over your head. It's not like you took it to buy yourself jewelry or anything."

A shadow passed over her face. "Anyway," she said with a smile, which even to his eyes looked forced, "now you know it all."

Though she'd been up front with him, he still had a feeling there was something she wasn't telling him. "Do you think your mother was aware you were taking the money?"

"Not at first." Sara brushed a piece of lint off her sleeve. "But she found out eventually when she needed the money for rent."

"I guess I'm not surprised she didn't mention it to me," he said. "It really didn't have anything to do with what we were talking about."

"Yeah, well..."

"I'm glad you told me, Sara," Crow said, his tone serious and intense. "Sometimes it helps to talk. If you ever need *anything*, I hope you'll call."

Her gaze searched his face and softness crept into her eyes. "Thanks for the offer."

Sara was a class act. She'd come so far in her

short life and had a great future in front of her. If only she would realize that some things in her past were worth keeping. "So, have you decided to call your mother?"

"I'm not sure," she said with a sigh.

"She wants to see you." He leaned forward and took her hand. "Forgiveness frees us, Sara. Think about what God would want you to do."

Forgiveness frees us.

Sara sat at the table and stared unseeingly at the newspaper before her. Since her talk with Crow yesterday she'd been unable to stop thinking about the past. Crow believed she needed to forgive her mother. Little did he know it was the other way around.

Still, he'd specifically said her mother had wanted her to call. Sara had prayed for years that her mother would someday find it in her heart to forgive her. She had to call and find out if her prayers had been answered.

The door to the kitchen swung open and Sara looked up. She groaned to herself as James strode into the room. How could anyone look so happy at 7:00 a.m.?

Sara took a gulp of double-strength coffee. "What are you doing here?"

She'd tried to be cheery, but even to her own ears she sounded grumpy and out of sorts.

"Good morning to you, too, sunshine." Surprisingly James didn't seem to mind. He smiled and pulled out a chair, sitting down at the kitchen table opposite Sara. "You may not be smiling now but I guarantee you'll be on top of the world after you hear my news."

She couldn't help but see the unmitigated excitement in his eyes, and despite her fatigue from a sleepless night she was intrigued. "Okay, you've got my attention. Lay it on me."

"Well for starters, your latest is number five on the charts and still rising," he said, satisfaction written all over his face.

"Are you kidding?" Sara said. "Marketing thought it would be great if we made it into the top twenty."

"And the good news doesn't stop there. Are you ready?"

Sara smiled at the melodramatics. "I'm ready."

"*Entertainment Today* wants to do a segment on you."

"*ET* wants to interview me?" Sara's eyes flew open and she was suddenly wide-awake. "Why?"

"Be-cause," he said, in a laughing voice, "you, my dear, are as we say in the industry, red-hot."

"James Smith, you are simply the best." She laughed with pure joy. "What would I do without you?"

"Sara." His eyes darkened and his voice grew

husky. He reached across the table for her but she sat back effectively moving beyond his reach.

"You've done a great job as my publicist, James," Sara said. "I really appreciate all you've done."

"But?" James said.

She smiled brightly, pretending not to understand. "There was no *but* in what I said."

"Yes, there was." His smile dimmed. "Let me finish your sentence. 'You've done a fabulous job as my publicist, James, *but* that's all you are to me.'"

"You're a good friend, James." She hated to see the pain in his eyes and to know she was the cause.

"But that's all."

Sara lifted one shoulder in a helpless shrug. She couldn't lie to him, or to herself, any longer.

"That's what I thought." His voice was heavy with resignation. "At one time I hoped—"

"James, don't," Sara said softly.

"It's him, isn't it?" James's gaze searched her eyes. "Your hippie bodyguard?"

"This isn't about Crow," Sara said. "If I could have picked a man to fall in love with, it would have been you. We work in the same industry, we have a lot of the same friends but..."

Though she wanted to be truthful, Sara also wanted to be kind. But how do you tell a guy without bruising his ego that the spark isn't there? That his kisses leave you cold? That your heart belongs to another?

She started to speak but James waved her silent.

"I understand perfectly." He paused for a long moment. "I guess I just need to know how this is going to affect our professional relationship."

"It's not," Sara said immediately. "You *are* a terrific publicist, James. I don't want to lose you."

His lips quirked up, and even if his smile didn't quite meet his eyes, she had to applaud his composure. "You just keep that in mind when my contract is up for renewal and I ask for more money."

Money.

Sara's smile faded. In the excitement she'd almost forgotten she'd decided to call her mother. Regardless of what Crow said, Sara was still not sure how her call would be received.

"Sara?" James's brows drew together. "What's the matter?"

She swallowed hard at the kindness in his tone. "My mother wants to see me."

"Your mother?" If she'd have told him Dr. E. wanted her to sing with him on his next rap album, James couldn't have looked more surprised. "Why?"

"Mend fences." Sara forced a light tone, wishing it were only that simple. "Do the mother-daughter reconciliation thing."

"I don't think it would be a good idea," he said.

"Why do you say that?" Sara fought to keep her tone civil, though it irritated her that he could dismiss the possibility with less thought than it took for him to select a tie.

"She's not the type of woman I think you should be associating with."

"James, think what you're saying," she said. "This is not just some strange woman. This is *my mother.*"

"I realize that," he said smoothly, using a tone usually reserved for a recalcitrant child. "But from what you've told me, you two are as different as night and day. And you've never been particularly close."

She had no reason to be irritated. After all, he was only parroting what she'd told him. What she'd in fact believed until she'd taken time last night to look back on her childhood with a more open mind.

"I want to see her," Sara said.

"I can't stop you," he said.

"No, you can't." She lifted her chin.

"I'm not the enemy, Sara." James's gaze met hers.

She could see the sincerity and caring in his eyes. Somehow that hurt even more. "Please understand. I have to do it, James."

"I won't give you my blessing," he said.

Chapter Seventeen

Crow dropped the last of the magazines into his apartment building's Dumpster and breathed a sigh of relief. Finally he'd be able to walk from the kitchen to the bedroom without stepping over piles of paper.

Still, he couldn't complain. Taking the time with those articles had been well worth it. They'd led him to Deanna and he'd solved the mystery of who'd been writing the notes.

Dusting off his hands, he headed up the three flights of stairs. He should be relieved but instead he was on edge. His normally infallible intuition told him something was not right and, try as he might, he couldn't ignore the feeling.

At the top of the stairs Crow turned the corner.

He stopped short at the sight of the dark-haired woman outside his door.

"Raven?"

She shoved a piece of paper and a pen back into her purse. "Oh, Sal. I was just going to leave you a note."

"Two visits in one week?" He raised a brow. "Should I feel honored?"

"You can if you want," she said. "But in the meantime, could you open the door? I'd rather talk inside."

She glanced around, an uneasy expression on her face. It was as if she expected someone to leap out at her any second.

His gaze followed hers and he saw the place through her eyes; from the bare light bulb that cast an eerie dim yellow glow to the scarred walls and the frayed carpet. It only confirmed that his recent decision to move was the right one.

Crow opened the door and let her enter in front of him. Once inside he automatically locked and dead-bolted the door behind him.

"Have a seat." He gestured to the couch.

Raven's gaze slid around the room. "I must say I'm impressed. The place looks one hundred percent better than last week."

"Better watch it." Crow smiled and plopped into a chair. "I might decide not to move."

Her eyes brightened and he could almost see her

ears perk up. "Move? Surely I didn't hear you correctly?"

"Actually I've decided to take a look at that house in Hazelwood you told me about," he said. "Unless you think I'd be a fool to let this impressive apartment go."

"Puh-leeze." Raven rolled her eyes. "You'd be a fool to stay. I think I've got that Realtor's number in my purse."

She searched her bag, and just when he was about to tell her to not bother, she pulled out a piece of paper that included not only the name and phone number of the listing agent but a picture of the house and the room dimensions.

He took it from her, unable to believe his luck. It was like a sign from heaven.

"It's got a picket fence." He stared in disbelief. "I never thought I'd find a house with one."

Raven stared curiously. "I never knew you were a picket-fence fan."

"I'm not," he said, folding the paper and shoving it into his pocket for safekeeping. "Sara is."

Raven's eyes widened and her lips curved upward. "Are you telling me you two are…?"

"Don't get your hopes up," he said quickly. "We're not anything…yet."

"But maybe in the future?"

He shrugged. "I hope."

"Sal," she squealed, and popped out of the

chair flinging her arms around his neck. "I'm so happy for you."

He peeled her arms off his neck and stood, wondering if he should have said anything. He moved to the window and stared unseeing at the brick wall of the building next door.

Crow never talked with anyone—much less his sister—about his personal life or feelings. But he found himself in need of some womanly advice, and Raven knew Sara. Plus, by the way her eyes were gleaming, she was anxious to help.

"I love her," he said matter-of-factly. "I think she loves me, too. But for some reason she's holding back. At first, I thought she was just mad because I hadn't told her I was an undercover cop."

"Didn't I tell you?" Raven said with a smug expression. "Women don't like to be lied to. I'm surprised—"

"Raven." He put a stop to her I-told-you-so ramblings before she really picked up steam. "Can we stick to my question please?"

A puzzled frown furrowed her brow. "What question is that?"

He smiled to himself. Even as a child she'd been easy to distract. "Her mother says she's always had a problem with long hair. But my hair is who I am."

Her gaze turned sharp and assessing. "Are you sure?"

"What do you mean?"

"If I remember correctly, you only adopted that look so you'd fit in with the drug dealers and junkies."

"That's true." He thought for a moment. "But still, she needs to love me for who I am."

"Maybe." Raven shrugged. "But is that who you really are, Sal? If not, why hold on to that image?"

"Who says I want to?" he growled.

"I still see the long hair," she said.

"I got it cut."

"You got it trimmed, not cut."

"Forget the hair," he said. "I don't even know how we got started on that subject."

"You brought it up," she said pointedly.

"Did I tell you I found out who was sending Sara threatening notes?" he said, deliberately steering the conversation in a different direction. "It was a woman she'd been friends with in junior high who turned out to have an ax to grind. But it could have been worse. It could have been some crazy guy out to get her."

"I have to tell you, I'm glad it was a woman," Raven said. "Because Sara and I were talking one day and she mentioned she had this enemy, some guy named Gary Burke. I meant to tell you but I kept forgetting. I would have felt terrible if he'd turned out to be the stalker."

"Gary Burke?" Crow frowned. "She said he was her enemy?"

"What does it matter?" Raven said, staring at him. "You already found the person who wrote all those notes, right?"

I sent one lousy note.

Crow stilled. That was it. That was what had been nagging at him since he and Dee had talked. She'd only said "note." Not "notes."

His heart pounded. If Dee didn't send the other notes, someone else did.

That meant the stalker was still out there.

And that Sara was still in danger.

Chapter Eighteen

Sara took a long sip of her iced tea, tempted to make another inane comment about the weather. If she'd thought making that call to her mother and setting up this meeting was hard, trying to talk to someone she hadn't seen in ten years was next to impossible.

They'd agreed to meet at a local restaurant, and on the way there, Sara had found herself wondering if she'd even recognize her mother. Thankfully that hadn't been a problem.

She glanced across the booth through lowered lashes. Crow was right; the physical similarities between mother and daughter were striking.

"That's a lovely dress," her mother said.

She glanced at her mother's tailored linen. Obviously they'd moved from the weather to clothes.

"I like yours, too," Sara said. "It's different than the kind of stuff I remember you wearing when I was a kid."

The moment the words left her mouth, Sara wished she could have them back. The last thing she'd wanted to do was to start off this meeting being negative.

Surprisingly her mother's lips quirked.

"Spandex just doesn't appeal to me anymore." Her mother's mouth twisted in a wry grin. "I guess I've grown more conservative in my old age."

"You're not old," Sara said automatically.

"Forty-four next month."

Sara thought for a moment. "The tenth, right?"

"I'm surprised you remember."

"There's a lot I remember," Sara said. "And just as much that I wish I could forget."

Her mother's gaze met hers. "And I'm sorry for that. I know that I wasn't a good mother to you."

Sara hesitated. How do you disagree with something that's true?

"I loved you and I certainly wanted to be, but I didn't know how." Without warning, her mother stopped and let out a long audible sigh. "No, I swore I'd be honest today. I was too focused on the men in my life to be a good mother."

Good manners told Sara she should protest, tell her mother that she was being too hard on herself. And to a certain extent that was true. She'd known her mother had loved her, and there had been good times. But on the other hand, if they were being honest, so often her mother hadn't been there for her.

"What are you thinking, Sara?" her mother said softly. "You can tell me."

"Why did you leave me?" she blurted out. "You said we were best friends. You never called, or wrote, or anything."

Tears pushed against the back of Sara's lids, and even though she'd voiced the question she longed to ask for ten years, it was all she could do not to bolt from the restaurant without waiting for the answer.

"I did it for you." Her mother reached across the table and took her hand. "And that's the truth. I thought it would be easier if it was a clean break. When I was younger, my mother ping-ponged in and out of my life so much I didn't know *where* I belonged. I couldn't do that to you."

"I thought you didn't love me anymore." Sara swallowed hard against the lump in her throat.

"I never stopped loving you." This time it was her mother's eyes that filled with tears. "How could I?"

"It was my fault Gary beat you up."

Her mother frowned. "That had nothing to do with you."

"Mom, don't lie to me now," Sara said. "I

know Gary found out that I'd taken forty dollars from his wallet and took it out on you. And I can't begin to say—"

"Forty dollars?" her mother interrupted. "What are you talking about?"

Maybe this was part of her penance, Sara decided, having to admit out loud what kind of person she was.

"I wanted a new dress for that freshman dance more than anything. And you said no." Sara tore the paper napkin that had been on her lap into tiny shreds. "I couldn't believe it when you let Gary have the final say. He had plenty of money in his wallet and you had to know he'd just blow it all on gambling and booze anyway."

Her mother stared as if she was hearing it all for the first time.

Sara swallowed hard and continued, suddenly anxious to get it all off her chest. "That's when I decided to borrow the money. I figured he'd never miss it and I could pay it back over time from my baby-sitting money."

A strange expression moved across her mother's face. "All these years you've thought that's why I got hurt? And that's why I didn't come for you?"

Sara nodded, lowering her gaze to the wooden tabletop.

"Oh, baby, I'm so sorry." Her mother reached

over and squeezed Sara's hand. "Sara, look at me."

Sara lifted her gaze and the wall she'd built around her heart melted at the love in her mother's eyes.

"What happened that morning had absolutely nothing to do with you."

"Mom, don't…"

"Listen to me. It had nothing to do with you." The words rang with an unexpected sincerity and her mother's gaze was firm and direct. For the first time Sara wondered if she could have been wrong all these years. Maybe it hadn't been her fault.

"I don't know if you were aware of it, but Gary and I hadn't been getting along for weeks. Every time we went out, he paid attention to every other woman but me. Finally I'd had enough." Her eyes darkened with the pain of remembering. "When I told him that morning to pack his bags he went crazy."

"He'd found out the money was missing, hadn't he?"

"He hadn't even picked up his wallet from the coffee table."

"Why was he so upset then?" Sara frowned. "It wasn't like he couldn't have gotten his own place."

"I think he didn't like being told to leave," she

said. "And the fact that there was another man in the picture."

"There was?" Sara said in surprise.

"Mike Richards. A guy I worked with at the time." Her mother stirred the sugar in her tea round and round. "Anyway, I'd never seen Gary so angry. He started in on how I'd always thought I was too good for him even though I was nothing but a two-timing..." Her mother's voice trailed off and she fluttered one hand in the air. "You get the picture."

Sara could only stare. Could it possibly be true that the money hadn't played any part in what had happened? "You're not making this up, are you?"

Her mother wiped the tears from her eyes and laughed. "Even I couldn't make up something like this."

"All these years I thought he'd hurt you because of me," Sara said.

"Even if your taking the money *had* caused Gary to blow, it would still have been my fault. I knew how mean he could be. I should have never brought him into our lives in the first place." Her mother shook her head. "Actually I was more worried about him hurting you rather than me."

"We barely talked," Sara said. "I tried to stay out of his way as much as possible."

"I know you did," Ilene said. "But you had to have been aware of his fascination with you."

"Fascination?" Sara rolled her eyes. "Dee and I thought he was a perv. Do you know once he offered us each ten dollars if we'd sunbathe topless?"

She and Dee had laughed at the offer, too naive at the time to be really afraid.

"I didn't know that." Her mother's lips tightened. "But why am I not surprised? Gary thought you were the most beautiful 'woman' he'd ever seen. It irritated him that you wouldn't give him the time of day."

All this time Sara had attributed her being taken out of the only home she'd known as an act of punishment. Now she could see that God had gotten her out of there in the nick of time.

"It was a blessing in disguise," Sara murmured.

"It turned out to be a blessing in disguise for me, too," her mother said softly. "Eventually it forced me to look at myself and where I was going. It took me quite a while to get myself on track, but at least I knew *you* had a good life."

Sara lifted a brow.

"Your foster parents sent me regular updates," she said. "I told them not to tell you."

"I wish I would have known."

"It was better you didn't," Ilene said matter-of-factly, signaling the waiter for more iced tea. "Being a teenager is hard enough without having a screwed-up mother to contend with."

"You weren't screwed up," Sara said.

"Thanks, but actually I was. Big-time." Her mother's voice took on a forced casualness. She gave the waiter a bright smile and held out her glass for a refill, as if grateful for the interruption.

Sara covered her glass with her hand and shook her head. Not until the waiter had moved on to the next table did her mother continue.

"I was a terrible mother." Her mother slowly sipped her tea while two spots of pink colored her cheeks. "But I am sorry. Truly sorry."

Sara swallowed hard against the hurt and anger welling up inside her. She'd prayed before she came that she and her mother would both have the courage to speak from their hearts. The question now was where did they go from here?

Forgiveness frees us.

She couldn't say that what her mother had done hadn't hurt, but how could she not forgive her? After all, Sara had made her share of mistakes along the way, too. And God had always forgiven her.

"I want you to know something." Sara leaned forward and pinned her mother with her gaze. "In spite of everything, I still love you."

Tears filled her mother's eyes.

"And…I forgive you." Sara's voice cracked with emotion. "I hope you can forgive me, too."

"Of course I forgive you. Though I'm not sure

what for.'' Tears slipped down Sara's mother's cheeks. ''And I'd like it very much if we could be friends.''

Sara smiled and she couldn't remember when her heart had felt so light. ''I'd like that.''

''Will you two ladies be having any dessert?'' The waiter stood with his pen poised.

''None for me, thanks,'' Sara said.

''I'll pass.'' Her mother extended her hand. ''But I will take the check.''

''Mother,'' Sara said firmly, reaching out. ''I want to pick it up.''

''Mother?'' The waiter's gaze darted from Sara to Ilene and back again. ''She's your mother?''

Sara nodded and reached across the table and squeezed her mother's hand, proud to say the words. ''Yes, this is my mother.''

He shook his head in disbelief. ''I would have sworn the two of you were sisters.''

Sara's mother rolled her eyes and they giggled.

Gary Burke's corner booth allowed him a perfect view of the two women across the room.

He'd been following Ilene since he'd gotten out of prison last week, hoping she'd lead him to Sara. Today he'd hit pay dirt.

Gary had recognized Sara the minute she'd entered the restaurant. Pretty at fifteen, she was breathtaking at twenty-five. She still had that air of sweet innocence that he'd found so appealing all those years ago. He wondered if she could possibly still be innocent.

He discarded the notion immediately. All those magazine and newspaper articles made her sound like some kind of saint. But he'd known too many women to believe that kind of garbage.

Women. They were nothing but trouble. Look at Ilene. If she hadn't threatened to leave him, he never would have gotten mad. And he never would have ended up in prison.

Sitting in that cell, he'd had a lot of time to reflect on the unfairness of life. On people who thought they were too good for you.

His hand slipped into his pocket and he fingered the switchblade.

It was time the pretty little songbird and her mother were taught a lesson.

Crow sat in an office at the police station and stared at the file he'd ordered on Gary Burke. Though the guy had only gotten out of prison last week, he'd already disappeared. His parole officer thought he'd left the state, but Crow wasn't so sure. He had the sinking feeling that Gary was in St. Louis.

According to prison officials, Gary Burke had been obsessed with Sara and her career. His counselors had alluded to it as a type of "fatherly" pride, though the two weren't related. Gary's cell mate on the other hand had said laughingly that there was nothing the least bit "fatherly" about Gary's interest in Sara.

Crow's fingers tightened around the pencil, snapping it in two. If that guy so much as harmed one hair on Sara's head...

"Sal—" one of the secretaries stuck her head in the doorway "—there's a call for you on line two."

He punched the button and lifted the receiver. "Detective Tucci." He then listened for a moment. "Where'd they spot him?" His grip on the phone tightened until his knuckles grew white. The busy intersection was less than a mile from Sara's house. "I'm on my way."

"Problems?" The gray-haired secretary at the desk raised a questioning brow.

"I hope not," Crow said, rushing past her. "Not if I can help it."

Sara hummed as she arranged the flowers in the crystal vase. Tomorrow her mother would be coming over for Sunday dinner and she wanted everything to be perfect.

The doorbell rang and Sara glanced at her watch. It must be Meg. When Sara had called with the news that she and her mother had reconciled, Meg had insisted on coming over to hear all about it.

The doorbell rang again and Sara started to yell for Annie to get it when she realized Annie was out on a date tonight. She adjusted the last of the baby's breath and headed to the door.

"Hold on, Meg. I'm coming." Sara unlatched the chain, flipped the dead bolt and pulled the heavy door open.

Gary shoved her aside and walked past her like he owned the place. "Well, what a surprise. She answers her own door."

Her heart jumped to her throat. Why hadn't she looked before she'd opened the door? Sara resisted the overpowering urge to run, knowing he'd catch her before she'd even reach the door. It would only amuse him, and she didn't want to give him the satisfaction of knowing she was afraid. "It's been a long time, Gary."

"So you remember me," he said.

"You're not easy to forget," Sara said. Even though his dark hair was now short and tinged with gray, she would have been able to pick that face out of any police lineup. "What are you doing here?"

"Would you believe me if I said it was because I missed you?" His hand reached over to touch her hair.

She stepped back and fought to slow her racing heart. Sara wasn't sure what kind of game he was playing but she didn't like the wicked gleam in his eyes. "Get out."

"I'm not going anywhere."

"What do you want?" Sara lifted her chin.

"What'd you think of those notes I sent?" Gary answered her question with one of his own.

"It *was* you!"

His smile widened. "Pretty clever, huh? Spouting those Bible verses and all." His face darkened and he shot her a look so evil, a chill raced up her spine. "You ruined my life."

A band tightened around Sara's chest.

"You and that mother of yours." Gary reached into his pocket and pulled out a knife. A switchblade.

Sara froze.

The knife sprang open. "If it wasn't for you, your mama never would have left me. You think you're so pure, so stinkin' good, but after I get through with you—" Hatred filled his face. "So if you don't want that pretty face all cut up, I suggest you cooperate."

What he was saying didn't make any sense, but the threat was clear. She could scream but who would hear her? Her gaze darted around the room, looking for anything she could use as a weapon. A bronze sculpture sat on the side table, but it was out of reach.

"Gary, think about it." Though she wasn't sure

he'd listen to reason, she had no other options. "You don't want to go back to prison, do you?"

His eyes hardened. "Why would I go back there? What happens here will be just 'tween you and me. Unless, of course, you want me to pay a visit to your mama? And I guarantee if that happens, there won't be no doctors to save her this time."

He took another step forward, then suddenly stopped, his gaze narrowing to a point behind her.

Sara turned and almost collapsed in relief.

Crow stood in the doorway.

"Drop the knife." Crow's gaze remained locked on Gary. "Sara, go into the library and lock the door."

Sara didn't bother to ask how he'd gotten in the back way. She didn't care. He was the answer to her unspoken prayers. Without hesitation she moved to his side.

"I'll call the police," she said.

"They're already on the way. I'm Detective Tucci, Burke. St. Louis PD." Crow's voice rang with authority. "Drop the knife. It's all over."

"You're wrong." Gary shifted his gaze to Sara. "It's not over. I didn't get what I came for."

In the blink of an eye Gary lunged forward, knife extended. Crow pushed Sara to the side and grabbed Gary's arm. Gary swung wildly with his other hand, his fist grazing the side of Crow's face.

Crow countered with a direct hit to Gary's jaw. The two were evenly matched. Except Gary had the weapon.

"Run, Sara." Crow yelled as the knife slashed his shirt.

But Sara couldn't run. She couldn't leave Crow alone with such a madman. She had to help.

The two grappled for the knife. Sara darted to the side table and grabbed the bronze statue. Lifting it over her head she brought it down against the back of Gary's head at the same time his knife plunged into Crow's chest.

Chapter Nineteen

"Some people will do anything to get some rest."

The husky feminine voice was familiar and Crow's lips curved up in a smile even before he opened his eyes to find the worried face of his ex-partner, Angel Weston, gazing down at him.

"Angel, how'd you…?"

"Know?" She moved to the foot of his hospital bed. "It's all over the station. You know how it is when an officer goes down."

Her tone was light but her gaze kept straying to the IV tubing taped to his hand and the cardiac monitor they'd discontinued earlier this morning.

"It looks worse than it is," he said, pushing himself to a more upright position and grimacing against the pain.

"Yeah, lucky he used a switchblade," she said with the sarcastic humor he remembered. "They don't hurt at all."

Crow wanted to laugh but he didn't dare. The last thing he wanted to do was to tear his stitches. He glanced around to see what his parents thought of his former partner's humor when he suddenly realized they were alone.

"If you're looking for your mom and dad, they're in the cafeteria. I told them to go grab a bite," she said. "They didn't want to leave but I told them I had a gun in my purse and I'd shoot anyone that laid a finger on you. Except the doctors and nurses, of course," she added.

"You haven't changed a bit." This time he had to chuckle. "How'd you get in here anyway? My parents said only family's allowed to visit."

It had explained why it had been almost three days and he still hadn't seen Sara. But if they were letting friends visit...

"That's still the rule," she said with an impish grin. "But I told them I had something important to tell you. When that didn't work, I told them I was your wife."

"You're joking."

"Why would I make that up?"

"And did you really have something important to tell me?" he said. "Or was that a lie, too?"

Angel brought one hand melodramatically to her chest. "I'm shocked that you doubt me."

"I know you. Remember?"

"Too well." She smiled. "But I do have something to tell you, and as one of my dearest friends I wanted to make sure you heard it from me first."

He raised a questioning brow. This sounded serious.

"Jake and I—" she paused for effect and delivered her news just as the nurse walked into the room "—we're going to have a baby."

His mouth dropped open. Although Angel and her schoolteacher husband had been married for over a year, the idea that his tough-as-nails partner might want a baby had never occurred to him.

But now, seeing her face flushed with excitement, and knowing how much she and her husband loved each other, it seemed infinitely right.

"Angel, that's wonderful."

"So you're happy?"

"I couldn't be happier."

"Well, I should hope so." The nurse, who'd been silent up to this point, spoke. "It isn't every day a man finds out he's going to be a father."

Angel's eyes widened and her cough sounded to his discerning ears more like a laugh.

It was all he could do to keep a straight face.

"Well, sweetheart—" Angel moved to the door and cast him a conspiratorial wink over the nurse's shoulder "—I've got some errands to run. I'll give you a call later."

She pulled the door shut behind her and Crow leaned back against the pillow. It was nice to know that in a world of constant change, some things remained the same.

Sara couldn't keep the disappointment from her voice when she returned from the nurse's station and faced Meg's questioning gaze. "His condition has been upgraded to good, but they still say only family is allowed to visit."

"I'm sure it won't be long before you can see him," Meg said soothingly.

"It's been three days already. If they didn't have that guard at the door," she said, "I'd go in regardless of what the nurse said."

Sara's gaze shifted to the door down the hall with the police officer sitting outside just in time to see an attractive dark-haired woman come out of Crow's room.

"Angel, haven't seen you in a while." The officer's voice carried clearly down the quiet hall.

Angel. Sara frowned. Crow had mentioned that name before. She was sure of it.

The woman and the officer talked for a few minutes before walking right past Sara and Meg on her way to the elevators. She was even more beautiful close up.

Sara waited until Angel got on the elevator before she returned to the nurse's station desk. An R.N. that had just come from Crow's room sat at the desk and looked up as Sara approached. "May I help you?"

"I'm here to see Crow, er, Sal Tucci," Sara said with more confidence than she felt. Still, if they let that woman in to see him, surely she could have five minutes.

"Are you family?"

"No, but—"

The nurse raised her hand, cutting off Sara's explanation. "I'm afraid visitors are restricted to family members only."

"But I saw that dark-haired woman come out of his room and I thought—"

"She's his wife."

"I'm afraid you're mistaken," Sara said. "Sal's not married."

The nurse's eyes grew frosty. "I'm afraid that *you're* the one who's mistaken. Not only are they married, but he just found out he's going to be a father."

"A father?" Sara's skin turned suddenly cold and clammy. "Are you sure?"

"Positive." The nurse smiled briefly. "Mr. Tucci said himself that he couldn't be happier. Now if you'll excuse me." She picked up a pile of charts and stood.

"Of course." Sara took a deep breath and headed back down the hall, her head reeling.

Her manager looked up from her magazine. "So, will she let you see him?"

"No, but it's fine. He's got everyone he needs here with him." Sara forced a brittle smile. "I'd only be in the way."

Raven propped her feet up on a pile of books and stared at Crow. "Are you okay?"

"Couldn't be better." Crow dropped an armful of clothes into a box and sat down. It had been almost two months since he'd been stabbed, and though he'd thought he was back to normal, moving all of his belongings from his apartment to his new house had shown him just how far he still had to go. But he'd found keeping busy to be a good thing. It kept his mind off Sara and how much he missed her.

"How's Sara?" Raven's gaze was sharp and assessing.

He forced a noncommittal shrug. "How would I know?"

"You've talked to her, haven't you?"

"Do you get some sort of sadistic pleasure making me regurgitate this stuff?" he said. "Every time I see you, it's the same questions. I'm surprised you don't have the answers memorized."

"Tell it to me again," Raven said, brushing a

strand of hair from her face with a lacquered nail. "I'm a slow learner."

Crow heaved an exasperated sigh. He could argue with her, but in the end he'd lose. "She sent me a card and flowers while I was in the hospital, but when I got out she was touring. I finally did reach her by phone. We talked and that was it. She was different somehow."

"And you told her I was your sister?"

"I've already told you I did." That part of the phone conversation had been the most puzzling.

"Tell me again what she said." Raven pressed.

"Something about nothing surprising her anymore," he said. "That she wouldn't even be surprised to find out I was married."

"I can't figure that one out. Why would she say that?" Raven said, a thoughtful look on her face.

"Beats me." Crow shrugged. "And it was weird. At the time, I thought it was funny. Like she was making a joke. I know I made her mad when I laughed."

It had been a difficult conversation. Sara had been distant, almost like a stranger. And every time he'd suggested getting together, she'd had some flimsy excuse.

"So you're telling me I shouldn't be counting on that bridesmaid's dress yet?"

"Save your money." Crow met his sister's gaze and as much as he regretted saying the words, he knew they were true. "The way it looks now it'll be a cold day in July before I ever see her again, much less marry her."

Sara pulled up to the curb in front of the address Raven had given her. She sat there for a long moment before shutting off the engine. She'd only agreed to come to Crow's housewarming party because Raven had put the screws to her. When she'd tried to politely decline the invitation, Raven had told her bluntly that after all her brother had done for her, couldn't Sara spare a couple of hours? Asking about what Angel thought of her coming had been on the tip of Sara's tongue, but she couldn't bring herself to say the woman's name.

Sara still could hardly believe he was married. Here she'd worried about his feelings for Raven, only to find out she was his sister. It was becoming harder to know who or what to believe.

But Raven was right about one thing. Crow had done a lot for her and coming to his party wasn't too much to ask. Sara squared her shoulders, and before she could change her mind, she got out of the car and headed up the sidewalk.

A white picket fence surrounded the manicured front yard and Sara's heart clenched. Though she loved her modern home with its tall ceilings and big windows, this traditional Cape Cod with its rose-covered trellis and brick sidewalk was her dream home.

Reaching the front door, Sara took a deep breath, pasted a smile on her face and knocked. Not sure if she'd knocked loud enough the first time, Sara raised her hand to knock again just as the door opened.

"Sara." A broad smile spread across Crow's handsome face. "It's great to see you. Come in."

Her breath caught in her throat. "You cut your hair."

Crow flushed and reached up with the tips of his fingers to touch the thick dark strands now cut short in the latest style. "It's a lot easier to take care of this way. Do you like it?"

Sara nodded, her heart doing somersaults in her chest. Like it? Always handsome, he now looked like he'd just stepped off the pages of a men's magazine. "What made you do it?"

He shrugged. "I don't know. I guess I was ready for a change."

She understood completely. He was going to be a father.

"Your house is lovely," she said politely, glancing inside and catching a glimpse of pale yellow walls with cream-colored trim and shiny hardwood floors.

"You have to come in." He ushered her quickly through the front door without waiting for her answer, as if he knew how close she was to bolting. "Let me show it to you."

The house was strangely silent and their footsteps echoed against the floor. "It's so quiet. Where is everyone?"

"Everyone?" He raised a quizzical brow.

"You know, the housewarming party?" She tried to remember exactly what Raven had said. Surely the woman would have told her if the party was a surprise.

He stared blankly. "I don't know what you're talking about."

Suddenly she understood. "You're not having a party tonight, are you?"

He shook his head. "Where did you get that idea?"

"Your sister." Anger at Raven's duplicity threatened to overwhelm her. Why would she have done this?

"Raven told you I was having a party?" He frowned, clearly puzzled. "Why would she do that?"

"I think it's perfectly obvious," Sara said stiffly. "She wanted to get us alone together."

"In that case, I'll have to call and thank her," he said with a grin.

"Thank her?" Sara didn't bother to conceal her disgust. "You're a married man. I don't know where Angel is, but I'd be plenty mad if my sister-in-law tried to set up my husband—''

"Stop right there," Crow interrupted. "Are you saying you think I'm married?"

"You are married."

"I may not remember my cellular number," he said, "but I think I'd remember saying those vows."

"Does the name Angel ring a bell?"

"What about her?"

"You admit you know her."

"Of course I know her," he said. "What's she got to do with anything?"

"And she's pregnant, isn't she?" Sara pressed on, wanting to box him into a corner, so he'd have to admit the truth. She wanted to hear him say he'd lied, so her heart could once and for all break in two.

"How'd you know that?"

"With your child."

"Mine?" A look of horror that would have been comical at any other time flashed across his face. "No way."

Sara couldn't hide her disappointment. What kind of man would deny his own child? "Then whose would it be?"

"My money would be on her husband, Jake Weston."

"Her husband?" Sara's mouth dropped open

and she shut it with a snap. "I thought *you* were her husband."

"That was your first mistake." He burst out laughing, and it was all she could do not to smack him. "Angel used to be my partner on the force. Whatever made you think we were married?"

"The nurse at the hospital said you were." Sara paused. "Why would she tell me something that wasn't true?"

"Maybe because—" Crow's grin turned sheepish "—Angel told the staff she was my wife so she could get in to see me."

"And the baby?"

"Angel wanted to tell me in person that she and Jake were having a baby. The nurse came in just as she was giving me the news."

"So you're not married."

"Not yet," Crow said. His gaze traveled over her face and searched her eyes. "But I do have someone in mind. I'm just not sure she'll have me."

Her heart jolted. The very air seemed electrified.

"You can be a bit overbearing at times." Sara's gaze never left his face.

Crow put a large hand to her waist and drew her to him. "But I'm good with children and animals."

His breath was warm against her cheek and her heart raced. It was all she could do to maintain her composure. Over his shoulder Sara noticed a red leash lying on a chair. "You never told me you had a dog. I know we talked about dogs, but you never said you had one. Have you had it long?"

She shut her mouth, all too aware she was nervously rattling on about nothing.

Crow smiled indulgently. "Wait until you see her."

He whistled, and in a matter of seconds a ball of honey-and-white fur barreled into the room, skidding to a stop at his feet.

"Why, it's a collie." Sara crouched down and held out her hand. The puppy came to her without hesitation. "She likes me."

"Of course she likes you," Crow said, his gaze meeting hers. "I bought her for you."

Sara's heart began to sing. "Your house has a white picket fence."

He nodded. "It was part of your dream."

"You've got it all figured out, don't you?"

"I love you, Sara. I want you to be my wife."

She stepped forward and brushed back a tousle of hair from his forehead. "You know I loved you even with your long hair."

He smiled. "I didn't need it anymore. I'm not going back undercover. I've decided to leave the force and start up my own security business."

"So you'll be home at night?"

"Should be. Why?"

"I thought it might be fun to start working on another part of the dream. Those two point five children?"

"I'd be glad to get started on that as soon as I've got a ring on your finger and the minister pronounces us husband and wife. That is, if you agree to marry me."

"How can I say no?" she said. "I love happy endings. And if I marry you, a happy ending is guaranteed."

"You can count on it," he whispered.

His lips met hers and the blood pounded in her brain, leapt from her heart and made her knees tremble.

Happy ending?

Sara smiled and lifted her face for another kiss.

Guaranteed.

*   *   *   *   *

Dear Reader,

When I wrote my second novel, *Undercover Angel*, I never dreamed that Angel's partner on the police force would return to have a book of his own. But in the end he proved to be too interesting a character not to see again.

And so, Crow is back. He still has long hair, his bad attitude and his unwavering dedication to the job at hand. We know he'll protect Sara. The question is, can he protect his heart in the process?

I hope you enjoy this book. And if you still haven't had enough of Crow and Sara, you can see them again. All you need to do is be sure and read my next book from Love Inspired!

Cynthia Rutledge

Next Month
From Steeple Hill's

Love Inspired®

A BUNGALOW
FOR TWO

by *Carole Gift Page*

Book #3 in
THE MINISTER'S DAUGHTER
miniseries

To escape her troubles, Frannie Rowlands finds sanctuary in an oceanside bungalow and becomes inexplicably drawn to her mysterious neighbor after he heroically comes to her rescue. Can their faith in God—and in each other—help them pave a loving future together?

Don't miss
A BUNAGLOW FOR TWO
On sale December 2001